OLD ED 6

Old Ed 6
Loren W. Christensen

Cover and interior design by Kamila Miller   kzmiller.com

ISBN: 9798386913649

First Edition

OLD ED 6

Loren W Christensen

Acknowledgements

A big hug to my wife, Lisa, a keen-eyed editor, veteran martial artist, and tolerant of my bleeding all over our Mac keyboard.

Carrie Woolfrey, close friend, scholar, healer, and editor.

Kevin Faulk, friend, editor, and a combat veteran of the war in Afghanistan

Kamila Miller for her consistently excellent cover design, interior layout, and advice.

"Chick Norris" with 4-inch spur

War Hammer with 4-headed face and a 4-inch spur

Old age is an island surrounded by death.

— Juan Montalvo

Chapter 1

Ed jerked awake, alert and clear-headed, his fight-or-flight juices pumping through his 77-year-old body. He twisted around in his brown leather recliner and looked across the dark room at his nightstand clock, 3:09 a.m. Ed was wide awake but didn't want to get up; there wasn't anything to do this time of night, and the room was freezing. He pulled the old quilt up to his neck, stuffed his hands into his sweatshirt's kangaroo pocket, and looked through the sliding glass doors onto his balcony.

Why did he awaken so abruptly?

Oh yeah, the terrible dream. All had been dark, Ed remembered, and the black underscored the sounds of disembodied screams and shrieks and beseeching and palpable fear.

He swallowed noisily, remembering one chilling particular of the dream, the thing that yanked him awake—he knew the people screaming.

Ed took a few deep breaths, slowly releasing them, the cold turning them to white fog, as he endeavored his body to let go of the tension. A minute passed before the memory of the dream fragmented, the pieces vanishing in all directions into the cold, dark room.

Last evening, he had turned his chair to watch the snow falling as he went to sleep, "snug as a bug in a rug," as his mother used to say when she tucked him in. He often slept in his comfortable chair, especially when it was storming out.

The vertical bars that supported the horizontal railing at the edge of the balcony, six stories above the ground, allowed him to see the dozen or so towering spruce trees in the front yard's wide expanse that ended at the street. He liked watching the evergreens—dimly and eerily lit by the walkway lights—whip about on windy nights, stand stoically as the dense fog crept around them, and as was the case this night, droop from the weight of snow.

The snowfall was at least two inches high on the balcony's horizontal railing, an inch or so on the seats and arms of the two rattan chairs, and less on the cement floor. Wind gusts slapped some of the snow against the sliding glass door, where it stuck and—

There was a handprint on the glass.

Ed grabbed the wooden crank on the side of his chair and pushed his calves against the chair's leg rest to raise him into a sitting position. He stood and moved to the side of the glass door, scanning the small deck. The walls on each side separated each condo from the ones on the right and left and acted as a sound barrier. There weren't rock and rollers at the rest home, but some with hearing issues did play their radios and TVs loudly. Not one of them, the youngest 67 years, could slip around the dividers without falling to their death.

Was it really a handprint?

Ed couldn't see it from where he stood nearly flush with the door; he had to back up a couple of steps into the room.

Where was it?

Leaving the lights off, he moved over behind the recliner and bent down until he was peering over its back toward the glass. That's where I saw it, he thought. Right there.

He retrieved his Streamlight industrial/tactical flashlight from his nightstand and moved over to the glass door. He shined it from the side of the glass, below where he saw it, and above. It was gone.

He shut off the light and looked out at the falling snow. The flakes were pinging against the glass now, warning of treacherous driving for the morning working stiffs.

The handprint's disappearance was as startling as seeing it on the glass door.

A ghost? He had made a lot of them, seventy-four...maybe more. Seventy-eight? But did he believe in ghosts, in a spirit world?

He shrugged as he crossed over to his nightstand again, set down his flashlight, and switched on the lamp. Many of the oldsters here at Spruce Grove Rest Home talked about ghosts, most believing in their existence, a few mocking the idea. He stood next to his bed and sipped from his nighttime water glass. Why had he never thought about it? Denial? Fear?

Maybe he, of all people, should ponder it, considering—

A flicker of movement in his periphery snapped Ed's head toward the glass door.

The terrible face, no more than an inch away from the glass, was looking in, a finger pointing at something long and slender protruding from a damaged eye spilling blood and gunk down the man's cheek.

The mouth was moving, the voice muffled by the glass. He couldn't decipher the man's words, but his tone was…accusatory.

Ed knew what the long slender thing was: a seven-inch nail. He had stabbed the man's eye by mistake. He was going for a kill spot behind his ear, but Ed had screwed up; it was one of the few times he had done so. The man had turned his head at the last moment, which Ed realized too late, and the nail punched through his eyeball all the way to his brain matter.

It killed the dope seller, Ed's assignment, but his work performance disappointed him. He was a highly experienced professional; there was no room for defects, even those that got the job done anyway.

The man at the glass door kept repeating the same incoherent words, his eye leaking, his mouth twisting in pain and accusation. As Ed watched him, he felt something foreign to him, something he had trained himself long ago not to affect his mind. Fear. He understood it was inevitable in his work and, for that matter, in today's world. So he had trained himself to accept it, just as he accepted the morning, the night, and the beauty and ugliness of the human condition. By learning to acknowledge it and assume its certainty, he was never paralyzed by its presence, even when it was sudden.

That is, until now, when a target from one of his past jobs shows up on his balcony, his cause of death oozing down his dead-pale face as he struggled to accuse through the snow-splattered sliding door.

The finger pointing at his eye suddenly jabbed at Ed, its fingernail clicking against the glass. The man's mouth opened wide, then shrunk to a small O as if to whistle, then wide again. His mouth remained open for several seconds, his good eye bulging as if both were frozen. Then his mouth slowly closed, and his hand rotated until the long finger again pointed at the destroyed eye, his good one glaring with malevolence at Ed.

The finger swept back to click against the glass again, its aim at Ed. The man's mouth once more stretched enormously open, then shrinking to whistle-small.

Ed knew what the mouth was saying: *You. Me.*

The finger turned back toward the protruding nail.

You did this to me.

Without thinking about it, Ed retreated a step, the back of his leg striking the nightstand, sending a bowl of coins sprinkling onto the floor. He looked down, though it was too dark to see anything, then back at the glass door.

He stared at the empty deck for a long moment, the snow in the wind, the buildup on the railing a little higher than earlier, the space by the door where the dead man had stood—empty. Ed sidestepped, one bare foot feeling the coins' chill, and continued until he reached the hall door. He pushed a light switch that lit the balcony.

Ed crept toward it, not with fear this time but caution. He peered through the glass, noting the absence of footprints in the layer of snow. He slid the door open enough to let himself out.

The balcony floor—a mixture of flakes and ice crystals—simultaneously burned and froze the soles of his bare feet. He didn't care. He moved over to the railing and looked across the 3 a.m. snow-covered tree-dotted lawn to the street. The frozen air was heavy with quiet; the wind had abruptly slowed, but it still chilled him through his sweatshirt as it carried away his white breath clouds. An unwelcome thought punched into his brain.

What if he turned around and the dead man, the long nail projecting from an unseeing eye, was on the other side of the glass door, looking out at him, his condemning finger pointing, its nail clicking the pane?

Chapter 2

Ed's eyes fluttered open, his mind void of thought for a moment before he was aware of lying atop his still-made bed. The nightstand light read 6:16 a.m., so why was his small apartment lighted, and why were his fingers, bare toes, and face so cold? And why was there frigid air blowing on him?

He raised his head from the pillow. He often opened the sliding glass door on mild days and when his lack of cooking skills set off the smoke alarm. But for some reason, it was open wide enough for him to go out and in.

He sat up, remembering last night. Snow. The dead man standing on the balcony.

He stood, quickly scanned his small apartment, and then moved toward the closed bathroom door. He cautiously nudged it open an inch, then another, until he could determine it was empty. He moved across the room to the balcony door. It had stopped snowing, and it didn't appear there was more accumulation. He slid the door closed. His recliner was where it always was, his blanket bunched on the seat. Over by his nightstand, his change bowl lay on the floor, coins scattered.

"But when did I lie down on the bed?" he asked the room. "Why didn't I close the door?"

Not knowing what to think about any of it, he moved into the kitchen and dropped a capsule of Stormio into his Nespresso coffee machine. Actually, it was Moxie's. Ed preferred his old clunker coffee maker and his old school Folgers. He drummed his fingers on the counter, cursing its sputtering slowness, though it was faster than his coffee maker. Finally, he leaned back against the counter, savored the first sip—okay, that's pretty damn good—and thought about last night.

Was he losing his mind?

That thought terrified him. His visitor wasn't real, but the fact his mind had conjured it bothered him. Was it because he was getting old, or was it a byproduct of his chosen life? His memory, the increasing number of holes in it over the last two years or so, had gotten better the last few months. Several old-timers in the home recommended Lion's Mane mushroom, a supplement, so he tried it. It took only a couple of days before he noticed a new clarity in his thinking and a more responsive memory. He had no clue how it worked, but it did. And if—

Ed blinked several times and swallowed hard, feeling as if his heart were lodged in his throat. He had been dreaming before something awakened him. He remembered darkness, so thick no light would ever penetrate.

Terrible sounds.

That was it. Godawful sounds in the dense, tangible blackness: horrific wailing, piercing screams, and pleading. The voices, dozens of individual ones, overlapping, echoing—and Ed recognized each one. Not their names or the circumstances of why he terminated them, but how they sounded during their final seconds of life.

But that wasn't completely accurate. Many of the targets, if not most, he killed quickly, so fast that they didn't have a chance to gasp or moan. But somehow in his dream, he recognized each one—

The sound of a quacking duck pulled Ed from his confused thoughts. He moved over to his dresser and opened his phone to his messages.

Ed, get your little butt down here. I got your coffee poured and your muffin buttered. Lewis is regaling the table with a funny story about an air battle in the Korean War. That man can find humor in anything.

Ed smiled, imagining Moxie's 66-year-old fingers with the sparkly purple nail polish a blur of motion. She stayed over at his place two or three times a week. He was glad last night wasn't one of them. She would have probably run out of his apartment screaming, "Ed's having some kind of seizure!"

He didn't want to go down to the cafeteria with all the old people, but getting out of his little room was a must if he hoped to retain any semblance of his mind. Hopefully, it wasn't too late.

He stripped off his sweats and slid back his closet door. He slipped on his Tommy Bahama khaki sand slacks, pale blue Somerset short-sleeved silk-blend shirt, and his $179.00 SwiftKnit Derby shoes. The total bill for the look was over $450.00. It was good enough for the cafeteria. He had just picked up a wonderful pair of Tom Ford's straight-leg trousers for $623.00 last week, but he would save those for something special. He had always dressed top-notch for his jobs, sincerely believing that it was important to look nice when sending someone to their grave. He had pulled the plug on that work, so now he dressed sharp to look good for the ambulance crew should an aorta in his ticker blow a gasket. Plus, he loved the feel of nice threads.

Ed didn't like the word "retired." It made him feel old. He told Moxie that he was keeping his options open. "For example," he said, "I wouldn't say no to a part in a porn movie."

She had nodded vigorously. "I can see that," she said, nodding thoughtfully. "I surely can. Lead man and everything. But you couldn't leave your black socks on like you do with me."

He had been untruthful to her about his 30-year career. When they first met, he told Moxie he used to help people with their investments. One night she came to his apartment when he was moving some money around in his accounts. He inadvertently left his laptop open to one of his savings accounts, a healthy one. He saw her glance at it. If she saw the total, it would have confirmed his white lie that he was a successful investor.

Ed had been a high school English teacher before he began terminating those who needed terminating in his mid-40s. He liked being a teacher, but he didn't like the kids. "They're all spoiled and privileged," he told his principal. "What we need is a war big enough for the feds to reinstate the draft to teach the shitheads what sacrifice, pain, discipline, and serving is about, as opposed to shopping at the mall and taking selfies." His not-so-subtle comments didn't sit right with the principal, and a week later, they ordered him to attend a meeting with her and a district rep to discuss his opinions.

Ed headed for the door, stopping halfway to look out at the balcony. No one was peering in. It was snowing lightly again. He sighed and told himself he needed a vacation.

He stepped out into the hall and closed his apartment door until it clicked. His head was in the clouds a few weeks ago, and he forgot to listen for the sound. When he returned in the afternoon, someone had gone in and helped themselves to their toaster. Moxie was madder than a wet owl because it was hers. He didn't like toast anyway.

Ed suspected Ben. The old fart had been living in the home for about two years. He fancied himself a lady's man and worked at it every time one of them passed within a few feet of him. "If I told you that you had a nice chest, would you hold it against me, honey babe?" was one of his regular lines. Ed had only seen a couple of gals giggle; most looked disgusted and hurried on their way. Anastasia, a 250-pounder with a Russian last name Ed could never remember, got face-to-face with him one day and called him something in her native tongue. When Ed asked her later about it, she said it meant his mother abandoned him because she knew he would grow into a disgusting, obnoxious bastard.

Ed slept with Anastasia once, remembering that she had been so aggressive that he had been afraid for his safety.

A couple of weeks ago, someone brought a cake into the cafeteria for Ben's 92nd birthday. He told the few who gathered for him, "Old age is coming at a really bad time." One or two people politely chuckled. When Ed didn't say anything, Ben glared at him and snapped, "You're not gonna say somethin' smart alecky?"

"Okay," Ed said. "At eighty-two, everyone has the face he deserves."

"One thing about getting older," Ben countered, "is knowing someone is an asshole before they even speak."

Ed's mouth turned up in a faint smile that didn't reach his eyes. The hitman's dead gaze would have chilled Ben's bones if he hadn't been so stupid.

Clifford, a one-legged man of 86, looked at Ed and nodded his head toward Ben. "We getz too soon oldt, too late schmart." Ed fist-bumped him.

Ed double-checked the door outside his apartment, then commenced down the long hall toward the north end, picking up the usual sound bites of life behind the closed apartment doors. In 606, Bill's snores sounded like a chainsaw cutting through an iron pipe; in 609, Sadie and Sabrina, the 76-year-old twins, were bickering about something (Ed grinned remembering a long and exhausting weekend he spent with those two a few months back). Don in 612—everyone in the home called him "The Don" because he was Italian—had Fox News blaring loud enough to shatter windows on the 5th floor. Six fourteen, 615, and 618 were quiet. Either the folks had passed overnight, or they were down in the cafeteria eating a high-fiber breakfast.

The large double windows at the hall's end revealed heavy leaden clouds ready to drop more snow. Ed leaned his forehead against the glass and looked down six floors to the fenced-in chicken coop outside the kitchen. Four of the five hens huddled together, bobbing for feed, while the big black rooster—"Chick Norris," so named by Tommy, the head cook—stood near the coop intently eyeing something Ed couldn't see.

Ed pressed his forehead harder against the glass, wanting to find out what was so interesting between the coop and the side of the retirement home. But he still couldn't see—

Ah, it was a big, fat gray rat skittering through the snow toward the chicken coop wire. The rodent probably got his corpulence from the half dozen garbage cans outside the cafeteria doors or eating the chicken feed.

The rat scurried over to a jagged hole in the chicken wire wall, scraped his fat body through, and plopped unceremoniously onto the bark chips. "And here I thought you looked smarter than that," Ed said aloud, his breath fogging the glass.

He swiped his hand across it just in time to see the red and black rooster take two purposeful strides toward the rat, stop, and flap its feathers as if giving it one, and just one, warning. The rodent hesitated, calculating his odds of getting into it with the bird. "Figuring your odds of having to fight is one thing, Mickey Mouse," Ed said to the window, "calculating your chance of winning is another. I wouldn't bet on you."

Bird and rat simultaneously jumped toward each other, their bodies banging together a foot off the ground. The rooster's black wings flapped madly, claws digging at the rat's bloated belly. The critters parted just as quickly, pausing about two feet apart. The rooster commenced circling the rat, the rodent's head following. Ed could see the intent in the bird's eyes even from six floors up. He remembered his favorite wrestler, John Cena, telling an opponent, "You can run, and I will chase you. You can hide, and I will find you. We're gonna fight, and I'm gonna hurt you."

The rodent has those razor-sharp dagger teeth, Ed thought, but Chick Norris has those deadly claws and the dagger-like spur on the back of its feet. Ed spent two summers on Aunt May's and Uncle Charlie's farm in southern Oregon when he was a teen, and he had seen plenty of chicken and rooster versus rat fights. Only one time did a rat win, and that was because the chicken was bloody injured from a coyote bite the night before. Life is hard down on the farm.

Down below, the chickens had stopped eating to watch their lover boy defend them. The rat advanced. "You got more *cojones* than common sense, Mickey M," Ed said.

The rooster and the rat again collided in the air. The bird was bigger and heavier, so its chest bump sent the rat rolling in the snow. The rooster charged after it, and with a lightning-quick strike, a move most people wouldn't understand what they were seeing, the rooster stabbed the rat in the neck with its long dagger-like spur that protruded just above and behind his claws.

Ed owned a War Club with a four-headed hammer on one end and a four-inch metal spur on the other. The maker of the club had to have had a rooster's deadly spur in mind when he designed it.

The rat lay motionless for a long moment as the rooster watched from two feet away. The rodent suddenly stirred, and Chick Norris made a single hop toward it, wings spread, then stopped. The rat's four feet pedaled, kicking up little pieces of snow, then the chubby body stilled again as a small circle of blood pooled out from its neck.

Ed often checked on the chickens and rooster, enjoying their seemingly easy life. They huddled together in the cold, sought shade in the summer, and watched as one of the cafeteria cooks collected their eggs. Ed liked to observe the chicken's interactions with the rooster, especially how the big black and red bird ruled the roost. This was the first time he had witnessed a life-and-death fight in the coop.

He would wish he hadn't.

The rooster's head twitched right, left, up and down several times, then up again—and lingered there.

Ed pulled his head away from the glass. It saw me, he thought, though logically, he knew the rooster didn't look up six stories and see him looking down at him. But it seemed like it. Ed looked down again.

The rooster head-bobbed in a tight circle around the rat and then stopped. It looked down at its victim for a moment—to ensure it wasn't breathing?—then moved on to his post a few feet from where the hens had resumed pecking at the ground.

Chick Norris tilted back his head again and looked up at the window.

Ed sucked in his breath, jerking his face back from the glass. "No. You did not just do that," he said aloud.

He looked behind him to ensure no one was in the hall heading his way to the elevators. Clear. He looked back at the window, deciding not to look down again. Ed had long ago stopped feeling anxiety, let alone fear. But then, he hadn't had a rooster eyeball him before.

Six floors up, Ed couldn't see the rooster's bonelike spur that protruded like a thick dagger two to three inches from the back of its leg. Those two summers on the farm, he had seen roosters kill with it several times. He had forgotten about it until some 20 years later when he was in San Francisco, China Town. There, he saw an old kung fu master demonstrate a form with what they called a "rooster claw sickle." The idea had amused Ed as he remembered the barnyard fights he witnessed as a boy. The man sitting next to him at the demonstration explained that many Asian cultures had developed fighting systems based on animals, snakes, and insects. Ed found it fascinating, though he wasn't especially interested in the martial arts. He bought a rooster claw sickle to remember his trip.

Twenty-five years later, he used his souvenir in one of his early jobs. He had whipped the sickle down diagonally from high, snagging the target's carotid artery with the razor-sharp metal spur.

The man, Ed couldn't remember his name or what he looked like, responded much like the rat: he died quickly. That was always best. He never liked long, drawn-out deaths.

As always, he tossed away the rooster-claw sickle after the job. But he still had the War Hammer with its deadly spur. He had never used it, and, now that he was retired, he never would.

So many jobs, he reflected. Sometimes the orders were to prolong the final heartbeat. He'd do it, of course; orders were orders, but he preferred quick, like the man he did with the sickle and spur... No, that wasn't an early job. By then, he'd been working for a few years, doing at least three jobs every 12 months, sometimes four. So that guy must have been his... Damn. At least his 30th or 35th, give or take.

Ed shook his head at his memory or lack of it. 'Early job' and '30th' were far away from each other.

He looked at the window but not through it. No, that rooster didn't look up at him. Just my mind messing with me again.

The doctor prescribed medication a few months ago, an antidepressant to help his hint of dementia. It seemed to be helping, but recently he has been experiencing things, seeing things he knows aren't really there.

Damn.

He wouldn't mind some memory loss, especially a few of his 70-some hits. He wouldn't mind that at all.

He might forget some or all of them, but the demon gatekeepers at the entrance to Hell would know exactly how many.

No, he wasn't going to look down again at the coop. Besides, it didn't happen, anyway. He poked the elevator button and hoped Moxie wouldn't be too cross about his tardiness. The window was the last thing he saw as the door swished shut.

Chapter 3

Forty pairs of female eyes turned toward Ed as he entered the cafeteria; the ten pairs belonging to the men didn't. The youngest man was 67; the oldest was 97. Four of the women were over 99, and one was 103. The oldest liked to dance and play cards; sometimes, she told stories about the 18 months she and her mother were interned at Auschwitz. Spruce Grove could house 165 oldsters. They currently had 153 women and 12 men, consistent with the numbers since Ed had been living in the place.

The youngest woman was Gloria, 66, eating with two men by the fireplace. She loved men, always had, and saw no reason to slow down. She told Ed that of the six she had slept with in the home, two of whom lived with their wives, he was the only one she would say no to. "For example," she said with a twinkle in her eyes, "No, I haven't had enough." After he laughed, she added, "I thank the Lord every Sunday for gifting the geezers Viagra."

Their romps abruptly stopped when Ed and Moxie became an item two and a half months ago. Not one to mince words, Gloria got in his face one day when she stomped up to him as he helped the grounds crew rake fall leaves.

Ed liked working outdoors from time to time in the sprawling yard and garden area. He did it to clear his head, plus he and Carlos, the work crew boss, enjoyed each other's company.

Carlos stood over six feet, was about 60 years old, and muscular from hard labor. He spoke English without an accent despite being born and raised in Sayulita, Nayarit, Mexico. He told Ed that he graduated with a social science BA from Portland State University 15 years ago.

"What the hell, Ed," Gloria blared, by way of a greeting, interrupting Carlos and Ed's conversation. She stepped between the two men, her back to the gardener. "Are you ignoring me now just because you have a girlfriend?" Carlos looked over her shoulder and pretended to bite his fingernails nervously. "Why did you choose a goofy woman with a silly beehive hairdo and pointy glasses?" Gloria snarled. "Her personal style peaked in nineteen sixty-five, you know?"

"Gloria," Ed said. "I don't think it's kind of you to say such things."

Carlos made a 'that-was-weak' face at Ed and shook his head with disappointment.

"Kind!" Gloria almost screeched. "I'm not trying to be kind. What the hell do you see in the old bat? Dollars to donuts, she can't do to you the things I do. You nearly passed out last time. Remember?"

Carlos made a 'you-lucky-bastard' face.

"Gloria, you need to calm down."

Carlos extended both palms and vigorously shook his head. This time Ed snickered.

"You think this is funny?" Gloria managed, her entire body shaking with rage. "You... Damn you, Ed!" She scooped up a handful of dried leaves and threw them at him, most falling short, the rest lightly hitting his chest. "You're a bum, Ed! A cheap bastard bum!"

With that, she spun about and stomped through the leaves toward the Grove's front entrance.

The two men watched her pass two oldsters, turn partway around without stopping, and shout at the two women, "Yeah? Well, what the shit is good about the morning?"

"Senor Ed," Carlos said, affecting a thick Spanish accent and again shaking his head as if Ed were a hopeless case. "Telling an angry senorita to calm down works about as well as baptizing a cat."

As he entered the cafeteria this morning, Ed acknowledged Gloria with a slight nod, then quick-scanned the room. It was a survival technique he had done for years, no matter where he was. Most of the time, he didn't consciously know he was doing it, but his subconscious mind was taking in data, which had saved his bacon on several occasions.

It was always the same number of people for breakfast, but the faces changed over time. If he had to guess, a third of them had passed on since he first moved in three years back. New people with old eyes replaced them, each knowing, though some lived in denial, that the Grim Reaper had already circled their expiration date on his calendar.

Ed accepted that someday someone would replace him, and Hell would get a new inductee.

Moxie was sitting at the center table, one of 12 in the dining room, with Lewis, the Korean War vet, and three white-haired ladies. Ed smiled and nodded to several women at other tables greeting him verbally or giving him little finger waves and 'I'm available' smiles. With a blend of pride and irritation, Moxie told him once that Brad Pitt would get the same welcome.

"It's a curse," Ed said with an exaggerated sigh, pretending it was a terrible burden. "But, my beautiful Mox, the only thing that can top being your lover is my being one with a sparkly, talking unicorn." Moxie had rolled her eyes at that. Silly humor wasn't her cup of tea.

Ed observed a philosophy of caring and protecting any woman with whom he was lucky to enjoy a relationship. In short, he was faithful to the one he was with, despite opportunities that came his way so often. He had long ago stopped trying to figure out why or if it was a blessing or a curse.

Since Ed had been at Spruce Grove, he was never without fresh pie, baked bread, casseroles, peanut butter cookies, and many other goodies that would clog his arteries with plaque if he ate all of them. He was always a gracious gift receiver, accepting each dish with feigned shyness and a kiss on the giver's ever-powdered and rouged cheek. The baked goods had abruptly stopped once it was clear to everyone that Moxie was in his life now. He assumed she had put the word out that she was now in charge of his pastry intake.

He nodded at a table near the kitchen occupied by five women, three of whom he had known intimately at one time or another before Moxie. His nod didn't reveal any carnal knowledge as he knew she was scrutinizing his every gesture as she was apt to do, especially in the cafeteria and other gatherings at the home.

"Why are you late? Where were you?" she said by way of greeting.

Ed sat and scooted up his chair. He smiled at Lewis and the other three ladies. "I stopped at Seaside Beach on the way and did a little morning surfing." The three ladies laughed harder than the joke warranted, and Lewis flared his eyes and warned him with a head nod toward Moxie, which Ed took to mean she wasn't in the mood. Guys had to be united in the cold war between the sexes.

"Sorry, Mox," he said, patting her hand. "It was hard to get going this morning." She was wearing her ring with the walnut-sized amethyst purple stone in it.

She told him the first time she wore it, as she tilted her hand back and forth under his lamp to show the sparkles, "The stone sells for nine dollars and change on Amazon. But mine consists of an emerald-cut amethyst center stone bordered with ten round-cut diamonds and accented with two trillion-cut light purple amethysts, for a total of two point thirteen carats. It's crafted from high-quality fourteen-karat white gold and has a total gem weight of two point fifty-two carats. I paid a little under a thousand dollars for it."

She lifted her eyebrows when Ed responded only with, "Nice." She must have wanted another response because she was cranky the rest of the evening.

One of the cafeteria workers dropped a container of silverware, making everyone startle-jump except Ed. Laughter followed.

"You gonna play in the snow today, Ed?" Lewis asked.

Ed smiled at Moxie. "You want to have a snowball fight, my dear?"

"Only if I can put a rock in mine." She didn't smile.

"I hope they have fresh cranberries this Thanksgiving," one of the white hairs said, sipping from her cup. Her name was Toni, and she was ninety-four. She and Ed had never done anything. Ed didn't want to be responsible for stopping her heart. Besides, he didn't think she liked him that way or any other way, for that matter.

"Can you believe that holiday is only three weeks away?" one of the other ladies said, losing some of her chewed muffin as she spoke. "Oh dear," she managed before covering her mouth with a napkin.

"Hard to believe," Lewis said. "Three weeks away, I mean."

"Isn't it, though?" a white hair named Beth commented, playing with her fork.

"What was that?" Gladys asked, cupping her ear.

Beth repeated what she said, this time at an even lower volume. She never pretended to like the woman.

"It's snowing again," Gladys noted.

"Yes, it is," Beth said barely above a whisper.

"What?"

Take me now, Lord, Ed thought, sipping his coffee. Please. A lightning bolt, anything.

———

Thirty minutes later, Moxie and Ed were standing by the large windows in the recreation room, watching it snow. They had the place to themselves. She had been distant during breakfast, and he hadn't said much either, his mind still thinking about his late-night visitor.

"You, okay?" they asked simultaneously.

"You first, Mox."

She took a deep breath. Ed could see the wheels turning in her head as to how to say whatever she was thinking. He knew better than to interrupt a woman when she was thinking. But what if she was plotting?

She turned to him. "We've been together exclusively for about three months now, right?"

Nonono. Please don't mention marriage again.

Ed nodded. "Yes."

Looking back at the snow, she said, "I woke up about two a.m. last night thinking about you."

Well, coincidentally, I had a visitor on my balcony about then—a dead man with a nail in his eye that I put there a while back.

She turned to him. "I was thinking that I really don't know anything about your past. You said you helped people with their investments." He nodded, reading disbelief in her eyes. Uh-oh. "So tell me, Ed, can you simplify the words hedge fund, Franklin Templeton, and FDI inflows? Oh, and sovereign wealth fund?"

Damndamndamn.

Moxie tilted her head. "You look puzzled, Ed." She said it with the mock innocence women portray when they have one up on a guy.

"I…"

"Yes, Ed?" Again, with the fake innocence.

"I'm a little offended by the question. Are you baiting me? You think I'm lying?"

"I don't know what I think. Since day one, I've felt this aura emanating from you. It feels like…quite frankly, it feels like danger, and I don't know what that says about me and my choice of men."

Moxie was hardly the first woman to tell him that. One lady, her name he couldn't remember, said, "Sometimes your eyes are as cold as a grave on a winter's day." Another whispered, her lips moving against his ear after a rainy Sunday afternoon romp, "My Os with you nearly stop my heart, but what is it about you that scares me?"

To that one, Ed had responded with, "Maybe the thing that frightens you is the very thing that gives you pleasure." Ed thought that was a great response, but she didn't. She said she didn't want to be that person and ended their relationship. However, she knocked on his door a month later for a no-conversation booty call.

"Ed?" Moxie said when he didn't respond. "Did you hear me?"

"What? Oh, yeah. What do you mean when you say, 'I don't know what this says about me'?"

"I'm embarrassed to say."

Then why bring it up? Ed hated it when women wanted to talk about feelings.

"I'm attracted to it, I guess," Moxie said when Ed didn't ask. "It 'turns me on,'" she made air quotes, "as the kids say. It makes me feel safe. But it scares me at the same time."

"Scared? Of what? You think I would hurt you?"

"Who are you really, Ed? Why am I feeling what I'm feeling? I'm pretty good at reading people; you've even mentioned that a couple of times."

Ed looked up at the sky and followed a single flake to the ground, where it became one with the now three-inch-deep accumulation. "Okay, I wasn't an investor. I'm sorry I lied. But it was a white lie to avoid bringing up things that are complicated and unrelated to us."

"White lie?" She shook her head, her voice breaking on the word. "a white lie is still a lie." She studied his eyes, the lines of her frown deep. "Then, what is the tru—"

"I'll never tell you. I'm sorry. I know that's not fair to you, Mox, but I hope you accept it knowing I have a reason to keep it to myself. No one else in this place or anyone you're acquainted with who knows me knows the truth. That will remain with me."

Moxie's mouth had dropped open halfway through Ed's reply. Her eyes remained on his after he finished, and it saddened him to see them brimming with surprise, hurt, and tears.

"I'll tell you this much, Mox. Not telling you will keep you safe."

She looked off to the side, her hands clasped in front of her, her knuckles white. "That sounds like a bad movie line."

"I agree. I guess I'm asking that you respect my privacy regarding that part of my life. She turned back, her eyes now narrow with anger. He reached for her shoulder. "I'm sorry, Mox—"

She jerked away from his grasp and snapped, "What am I supposed to do with what you just said? Your words are hurtful, but the meaning between the lines is even more so. 'Go fuck yourself, Mox' is what I'm hearing. I…"

"I'm sor—"

"I swear to God, Ed. If you apologize one more time, I'll kick your balls—"

"Mox…"

She turned sharply and hurried across the room and out the door. Ed could hear her sobbing as the automatic door closed behind her.

Ed didn't want to go to his room, so he sat in a plush chair facing the window and watched the snow accumulate. At its current rate, it would soon be four inches deep in Spruce Grove's backyard. And if it were a typical Oregon winter, soon it would turn colder, changing from snow to treacherous ice rain. More money for the auto body repair shops.

He returned to Moxie's dramatic stomp out of the room. He thought her confrontation came out of nowhere, but he knew better. Recently, she had been a tad distant, not smiling at his quips and shrugging indifferently when he suggested two evenings ago that they go to the pho restaurant three blocks away for Vietnamese soup. When he took her hand yesterday, she didn't stroke it with her thumb as she usually did.

Mox's feelings toward him had progressively gone cold. Was it something he did or didn't do? It was one of those, no doubt. After nearly three months, she had figured out that he was only giving her the superficial, the surface Ed: polite, funny, snappy dresser, and a good conversationalist. He wasn't one to let people in, even his girlfriends. There was a reason: They wouldn't like it in. Even if the most adventurous woman learned a little of his history, she wouldn't like it. Leonard Cohen, his favorite singer, sings in "Waiting for the Miracle," *I don't believe you'd like it, you wouldn't like it here. There ain't no entertainment, and the judgments are severe.*

Besides, it's common knowledge in police work that it's almost always an angry and vengeful ex-girlfriend who snitches on the man to the police. He broke his rule once, and that was with Florence. She knew most of it, meaning not all of it.

He came close to telling Moxie some things recently. They had been sitting on his balcony, drinking tea, and eating cookies she had brought to his room. They had been sitting for about an hour, neither speaking for the last 15 minutes or so. He didn't know where she was in her mind. She had a son in Florida; maybe she was thinking about him. She had worked as a nurse at Good Sam Hospital in Northwest Portland for the last 24 years of her 35 in nursing. Maybe she was thinking about that and her life with her late husband, Gary.

Ed had been thinking about a job several months back when he knocked a man out with chloroform before using a Milwaukee Cordless Hammer Drill to bore holes through his kneecaps and elbow joints. He didn't kill him because the client wanted the target to suffer crippling debilitation for the rest of his life. Ed had to have total faith in The Organization that there was sufficient justification for that kind of specialty work. And he did.

So why was he thinking about it and feeling a little… He wasn't sure what he was feeling. Agitated? Yeah, a little. Destined to Hell? A little of that too. Would he go there despite his efforts to remove definite evil from the world? He didn't know.

He was the first to break the silence on the balcony, though he wasn't aware until after he had voiced his thought.

"Do you think I've been a good man?"

He continued to look out at the trees and was only partially aware of her cup stopping halfway to her mouth before she turned to look at him.

Later that night, she told him she knew something was on his mind because when she had set the teas on the table between them and a platter of cookies, he had continued to look out at the treetops without thanking her. His politeness was part of his charm, she said, and she could count on two fingers since knowing him when he hadn't said "please," "thank you," or "you're welcome."

She went on to say that some writers claim that charm is a deliberate act, a verb used to get something. "But I don't believe that," she told him. "At least it's not true with everyone. Your charm is part of who you are. You don't use it to get something. It's mingled into a delicious soup of kindness, humor, fitness, and joy for life. That's you."

Ed almost blew a gasket, trying not to laugh at that complete misread of who he was.

After he asked her the question, not completely aware he had done so aloud, he sat rigid, white-knuckling the arms of the rattan chair, his eyes wet, his gaze miles away.

"Ed."

"ED."

"ED!"

His eyes fluttered as if awakening, and he slowly turned to her, wondering when she had come to his room.

"My sweet man," she whispered. "There you are. My goodness. Where were you? Your eyes. They seem a thousand miles away. Or what's that thing they say about some soldiers? Their eyes have a thousand… Oh yes, A thousand-yard stare. But you weren't in the service, right?"

He looked down at his mug, no longer steaming. "Thank you for the tea and cookies." He didn't take one, but he did slurp his tea.

"It was hot when I set it down. I'll go zap it."

He quickly laid his palm on her arm, his eyes searching hers. "Please stay with me."

She covered his hand with hers. "Of course." She studied him for a moment, then, "Your question."

"Question," he said flatly.

"You asked me if I thought you had been a good man."

Ed frowned, not remembering.

"You seemed kind of far away when you asked. Do you remember?"

He turned and looked at the balcony floor.

"I haven't known you long, Ed... Look at me, please. Thank you. I know," — she patted the back of his hand—"I know you have always been a good man. The most wonderful man I've ever known."

Sitting in the conference room in front of the huge window, Ed shook his head, thinking about all that Moxie didn't know. And never would.

A bird, a crow, streaked toward the window, and just as Ed brought his hand up to protect his face against flying glass, it banked hard to the left and swooped upward, vanishing beyond the building.

"A hired assassin," he mumbled to himself. "They sent a bird to peck me to death, but it lost its nerve."

He started to get up, stopped, stretched his arms overhead, and yawned instead.

He turned back to the window and the snow-covered trees beyond. What an amazing knack Moxie has for reading people, he thought without humor. The last thing he saw as sleep swept over him was the return of the black-feathered assassin sitting on a swaying snow-ladened tree branch, looking his way. "A crow?" he said. "Is that all they think of me? I don't even get a raven."

Ed awoke at 10:15, still alone in the conference room, feeling better after his short morning nap and thinking it would be a good idea to stop by Moxie's room and make amends. He wasn't sure how to do that because he wasn't about to tell her his history. His presence may be enough. But probably not. You never know about the female gender. They're likable but not understandable at all. And he wasn't even sure how much he liked her.

Moxie's apartment was also on the sixth floor, two down from the elevator. Ed decided not to check on the chickens and rooster again and headed straight for her door. He had had enough of birds for one day. First, there was the rooster's chilling gaze, then the swooping bird outside the recreation room. He didn't do his special knock because if she were still mad, she wouldn't answer. He tapped it lightly, like one of the little ol' ladies.

No answer, and he didn't hear her rustling around inside. "It's me, the asshole." He thought that would get a half smile, and she would tell him to come in. But all was silent inside, unusual because her normal routine was to come up after breakfast and do her apartment chores. Maybe she's confiding in a friend about how frustrating I am, he thought.

Chapter 4

Ed scrunched his head deeper into the collar of his graphite-colored Norwegian wool and silk coat he bought in late fall from Saks Fifth Avenue for just under $2000. It hit him mid-thigh, which seemed like a good idea when it was 60 degrees out in October, but now that his knee joints were freezing, he wished he'd gotten an ankle-length one. He had two long coats back in his apartment, but he misjudged how strong the wind was today. At least his Gucci wool hat, $360, kept his head cozy. He might be freezing, but he knew he looked sharp, albeit shaking like a Chihuahua.

The falling snow wasn't quite at white-out conditions because he could make out Annie's Coffee and Goodies across the street and the Starbucks next to it. The oldsters at Spruce Grove had kept Annie afloat since "friggin' Shitbucks horned in," as Annie often referred to the monopoly.

When Ed returned to his apartment after knocking on Moxie's door, he found that she had taken her coffee cup, a jar of honey, and the batch of cookies she had brought over yesterday. The items had been sitting in their usual spot by the spices between the fridge and the oven, but somehow, she had missed the Nespresso machine.

He had decided he needed to go for a walk to get some cold air, stir his blood, and clear some of the ridiculousness out of his head, like assassin birds, dead people on his balcony, and a woman who suddenly needed to know about his past. So far, his walk had only made him cold.

The bone-numbing chilliness aside, he was enjoying the heavy silence and the aloneness of the empty, snow-covered sidewalks. It was two inches high on this street, but on the way here, the snow had collected in sporadic drifts a foot deep. The intersection traffic light next to him now steadfastly cycled through its colors, though he had only seen one vehicle pass through the intersection: a black and white police SUV.

The dead man on the balcony this morning had been a skier on the cusp of qualifying for the Olympics a year earlier. The Olympic

Committee had been investigating him regarding multiple complaints from women—unwanted touching, exposing himself in his hotel room: Harvey Weinstein-like antics. They had just decided to boot him from the U.S. team when his minor crimes escalated to violent ones. The vicious rapes occurred on a Friday and Saturday night in Switzerland. One was a teenager, a ski groupie, and the other a hotel maid. The maid died. The cops arrested him on a Sunday, two hours before he was to compete. It was big news, and then it got bigger when Daddy's money got him off scot-free.

Ed could only recall the skier's first name, Biff. Ed smiled at that, imagining the parents looking down at their newborn and agreeing to name him Biff. Oh, and he remembered that he had been 32 years old.

The first part of Ed's orders was simple: terminate the skier—Andresen, that was his last name—the way the courts failed to do. The specifics were to use a prize ski pole the sex offender displayed over his fireplace to terminate him with "extreme prejudice." Ed remembered chuckling when he saw the two words. The customer must have been an old military man or watched too many war movies.

Ed did as ordered. He plunged the ski pole, tip first, deep into the screaming man's heart, let him savor the pain for a minute, then rotated it a few times to rip and gouge the valves, aortas, and arteries. Once the man was dead, Ed was to write RAPIST/MURDERER in all caps across the man's forehead with a Sharpie, take photos of the dead man with a burner phone, and send them to the tabloids.

Ed shook his head. Funny what you think about when watching the snowfall.

Although he wore black Marco lambskin gloves with brown fur lining, his fingertips ached from the cold. He rubbed his palms together vigorously. It didn't help. He shrugged deeper into his Norwegian coat and crossed his arms, his hands in his pits.

He detected movement out of his left periphery. He didn't turn to look but rather kept his face toward Annie's across the street as he watched the figure in his highly developed side vision stop after rounding the same corner that he had come around about 40 minutes earlier. The person hesitated for a couple of beats—as one might do when they see something they didn't expect to—then continued coming his way.

Not a vehicle had passed since the police car, and the only sound in the hushed, snow-falling air was the traffic signal, dutifully moving from green to amber to red. Nor was there anyone else on the sidewalks: just Ed and the figure coming his way.

He couldn't determine if it was a man or a woman, but he could decipher that the gait was strong, confident, and sure-footed, even on the slippery sidewalk. They hesitated again—one second…two…three—then commenced in his direction.

Closer now, Ed could better see the heel-to-toe manner of stepping, most often a female trait, but the assuredness of the gait, bordering on a swagger, made it male. Ten yards away now, the walker hesitated—one second…two…then commenced walking.

Ed's face remained forward as if he were concentrating on something across the street.

The person hesitated about 15 feet away.

"I'm delighted to see you again, Pearl," Ed said, his face grinning as he turned to her.

"You dog!" she said, hurrying the last few steps, nearly knocking him over with her embrace. Ed laughed, patting her back. She leaned back a little, holding his upper arms. Her face had flushed from the cold and her happiness to see him. "And I thought I was being so clandestine. I even stopped a few times to make myself more mysterious."

"It was your nametag that burned you,' Ed said seriously.

Pearl looked down at her coat front. "What? I don't have—" She looked up to see his smirk. She laughed and slapped his arm.

"So how did you know it was me," Pearl asked, scooting herself comfortable in the booth at Annie's Coffee and Goodies. She looked around at the little café. "You quit Starbucks? No more chocolate Grahams?"

He shook his head. "I don't like their politics."

"I wouldn't have figured you would give two cents about that, Ed?"

"Stay unpredictable, right," he said. The 34-year-old hitwoman nodded. "To answer your question as to how I knew it was you, I got a whiff of Garance Doré: Bonpoint Eau De Toilette when you were about fifteen feet away."

"Oh, my God!"

"You told me once that your aunt would get it for you whenever she was in Europe. You said it was one of the five little-known perfumes in the world."

"Wow, a man who listens and can detect one of the world's five obscure scents."

"I have gifted a couple of ladies with a bottle over the years, a generosity that paid off with a divine carnal knowledge." Pearl rolled her eyes, which made Ed chuckle. "But seriously, folks, I have a great nose that has saved me a few times. Oh, and I can River Dance too."

"Really?"

"Sure, I can." He smirked and then caught Annie's attention as she sat down a slice of pie to a uniformed mail carrier sitting at the counter. "Two coffees and two pieces of your apple pie, Annie." He looked at Pearl to see if that was okay; she nodded with a grin.

"Be right over, Ed," Annie called back.

Pearl leaned toward him. "She's cute, Ed. About ten years younger than you, big boobs, probably makes the pies here, friendly without being false about it, keeps a tidy place, and smiled at you large when we came in and again just now when you ordered. I think you missed her first one."

"Nah, I saw it. Back to your perfume."

"You detected it twice now—"

"Four. Three times the last time we were together and today."

"Damn. You going to lecture me about never forming a routine?"

"Doesn't sound like I need to, now."

"You don't. I'll remember."

Annie crossed to them, carrying two steaming cups and two large pieces of apple pie. "The ice cream scoops are on the house. How are you, Edward?"

"I got one foot on a banana peel and the other in a grave, Annie. This is my friend...Jade. Jade, Annie. Best cook in the West."

The waitress smiled, nodded at Pearl, then punched Ed's shoulder. "And don't you forget it, Edward." She smiled at Pearl. "Watch him, Jade. He shouldn't be left unattended."

"I totally agree, Annie."

Pearl raised an eyebrow at Ed as the woman headed back to the counter. "She's yours for the asking, *Edward*. And Jade? Really? That's as good as you could do?"

He studied Pearl as she took her first bite of pie. They had kept in contact by email but hadn't seen each other in a while. Of course, she never said anything about the job in her emails, and he never asked. She sent a picture of a muscular bulldog once that she was thinking of getting but decided against it. "I'm not home enough," she wrote, meaning she was getting assignments.

There was a hint of change about her. Toughness? Yes. Edginess? Yes. Nervousness" A little. But it was her smile that was nagging at him.

It was polite and activated her mouth's zygomaticus muscles but not the orbicularis oculi around her eyes. Other times the zygomaticus pulled her mouth into a repeatedly fired smile, each disappearing as quickly as they appeared.

Those things were new, and it gave him pause. They could be from the job, the inevitable resultant aftereffects of terminating human lives. That wasn't unusual with new agents.

"How long's it been?" he asked.

"Five months, give or take. I've missed you."

"Have you been working?" he asked, then wondered, Are you working right now?

Pearl worked for Cull, an agency based somewhere near Seattle, similar to The Organization, where Ed had worked for three decades. The Organization was headquartered in Australia. When he first met Pearl several months back, she had been with Cull for three years but had only recently moved into field agent work. She had completed one job at that time, working with a coach.

"Two by myself," Pearl said after sipping her coffee. "And two with a partner who watched me without saying anything good or bad. The ones by myself were in Louisiana and Idaho, in that order. I just happened to be visiting my uncle on my dad's side in Missoula when Liam called."

"Is Liam White your main contact at Cull?"

Ed and Liam worked a job together several years earlier. Would he call him a friend? Ed thought. That was a complicated word to define in the business. Ed felt the Australian man was a friend until The Organization sent the Aussie to eradicate him, an assignment that didn't turn out well for the rusty hitman.

"Yes. I really like Liam. He doesn't treat me like a newbie or a weak female, and he has a way of correcting me and teaching me without it being condescending. I was very pleased when he told me that the guy who accompanied me to the two jobs gave me a glowing report."

Ed speared a piece of apple and collected a little ice cream on the way to his mouth.

He could see that Pearl was waiting for him to complement her. She continued when he didn't. "The job was in Helena. Liam said it was an easy one, a terrible woman who had deliberately passed AIDS on to eleven men and kidnapped a little boy, the son of one of the victims. I was doing okay on the assignment, but all of a sudden, it went to shit. She gave me this." Pearl pulled aside one side of her bangs to expose a four-inch pink scar.

She looks proud of it, Ed noted. He remembered feeling the same. But he was younger then.

"Happened three months ago," Pearl said. "It's taking forever to heal."

"I've got seventeen permanent ones," Ed said matter-of-factly, forking in another chunk of pie and ice cream.

"Scars?" Pearl asked wide-eyed.

"Lots more have disappeared over the eons. Want to see some? It will involve me stripping."

"I'm good."

"Thank you for not saying, 'Not while I'm eating.'" He waited for her smile to dissolve, then, "You said you were 'doing okay on the assignment, but then it suddenly went to shit.' The longer you do this job, the fewer 'suddenly' moments you'll get. Experience tends to eliminate their possibilities. But know this, they won't go away entirely. There are times you do everything right, but a 'suddenly' pops up anyway. When you're mindful, when you're in the moment, you can deal with it quickly and efficiently.

"Two years ago, The Organization lost two agents, both of them because they weren't in the moment. One had been drinking. He wasn't drunk, but enough that he didn't see the target retrieve a knife from behind his laptop. By the time he did—his fuzzy brain processed that it was a bad thing, and his muscles responded defensively—the target had already stabbed him in the chest and neck. The second agent who died was distracted by the target's figure and how she barely covered it. It was assumed that lust slowed his reaction to the gun suddenly in her hand."

Pearl made little circles on her empty pie plate with her fork. "Thank you, Ed," she said quietly. "What happens to the target when an agent falls?"

"With these two cases, I was sent to finish the assignments."

"With orders to make them suffer, right?"

Ed looked at her. A veteran agent would never ask that question because they would know the answer. Pearl's face blushed under his gaze. "What do you think?" he asked.

"It was a stupid question. Sorry."

Ed nodded, pleased that she realized her beginner's blunder. "When you catch your mistake, it means you're learning."

"Thank you," she said quietly.

She had been as giddy as a cheerleader when they drove to Seattle a few months back for an assignment. After he admonished her, she said she was just excited to have met him and to be actually going on a job with him.

Ed understood that, but he wasn't convinced that was all of it. She wasn't terribly young at 34, but her lack of maturity for the work was showing. He told her that her excitement wasn't an excuse for being flighty, almost giggly about killing a human being. Later that night, when he terminated two men who had been following them using a Hawaiian weapon edged with shark teeth, she had power puked all over the ground. That put a kibosh on her giddiness.

The front door dinged as two uniformed police officers wearing winter police jackets, blue scarves around their necks, and black gloves entered Annie's. They nodded at Ed; the younger cop eyed Pearl for an extra beat or two.

"How was your pie?" Ed asked, watching her sniff self-consciously, pick up her coffee, and sip, her eyes quick-darting toward the officers now ordering by the register. She looked at Ed and nodded. "Good. Just like mom never made."

"Not a good cook, huh?"

"She rarely did when I was growing up. Dad did most of it; he was good."

"He's passed; I think you told me."

She nodded. "I miss dad dearly. And now mom has had to learn to cook for herself." She smiled at the officers as they passed behind Ed, carrying 12-ounce coffees. The door dinged again as they left, a rush of cold air washing over the room.

"They make you nervous?"

Pearl lifted her eyebrows. "Uh, yeah. The shorter one was cute, though."

"Nervousness is a good sign. Overconfidence is worse than no confidence." He chewed his last bite of pie, his eyes noting that she was still moving her fork in circles on her empty plate. "Were you hypervigilant after your hits?"

She nodded. "Very. Watching my rearview mirror all the way back to Portland. I still do, actually. Just now, my heart stopped when those two officers came in." Ed watched her pick up her napkin and dab at her clean lips. "Do you, Ed? Hyperventilate, I mean, or get nervous after?"

"No."

"Really? Why? How could you not be?"

Ed looked at her so long that her face tightened and blanched. Her eyes looked off to the side and then, with apprehension, looked back at him.

"You wouldn't understand. If you stay with it, you will, but by then, it will be too late."

Pearl looked at him, her expression not understanding the words 'too late.' He didn't explain further, believing some things can't be taught.

Chapter 5

It was mid-afternoon, and Ed was sitting in his recliner, looking out the glass sliding door at the balcony. The snow had stopped falling, but not before it dropped another two inches on his balcony railing, making it about four inches high now. There wasn't a handprint on the glass or footprints on the balcony floor. That was a good thing.

He could see his dresser lamp reflected in the glass and Moxie's water bottle on the other dresser, half empty. She had last stayed over three nights ago, seizing the moment to talk about marriage, then getting perturbed when the only thing he contributed to the conversation was, "I know very well that I'm everything someone is looking for in a hunky man, but I don't think I'm ready."

He called her apartment on the way back from coffee with Pearl but still no answer. Barbs, staffing the lobby desk, said Moxie left around 10:30, but she hadn't seen her return. "But I'm not always at my desk. I stay busy all over the place, doing this and doing that and—"

"Did she say where she was going?" Ed cut in.

"Not a word. Moxie seemed unusually tight-lipped; you know what I mean? Did you two have a squabble? My late husband and I had some doozies let me tell you. One time—"

Ed quickly excused himself and grabbed an elevator.

Back in his apartment, he dropped a Stormio coffee capsule into the Nespresso machine. It was a goofy name, but it was good because it tasted like coffee should, not like the foo-foo flavors the younger generation liked.

He was too tired to wait for it standing, so he plopped into his recliner as the sputtering sounds of the machine commenced doing its task. A couple of minutes later, Ed began doing the sleepy head nod thing. Not wanting to nap, he shook his head awake, stood, and headed back to his coffeemaker as it spat out the last drops. He smiled, remembering a sign in the cafeteria that read, "Tips on how to fall asleep in a living room chair: 1) Be old. 2) Sit in a chair."

He sat back in his recliner, put up the footrest, and took his first sip. He thought about Pearl returning to Portland. She said she wanted to see her mother and him, but something nagged his brain. His gut was often right, which meant it was sometimes wrong. Assigning agents to terminate other agents was rare, but it did happen. He could think of a handful of times in the last 30 years, the last when his own boss from The Organization, a man he thought was his friend, came after him. The man failed, but it left Ed with a boatload of uncertainties.

The biggest was that his wall of subconscious denial that he would never be a target had crumbled. It was like how he felt after his first traffic accident at 67. He had driven for 45 years without a scratch on a fender. But after a woman crunched his passenger door in a parking lot, the denial wall that made him foolishly believe he would never be in a fender bender was gone, leaving him to drive with paranoia that it would happen again.

Was the absence of the wall why he felt a trace of mistrust about Pearl today? 'Just because you're paranoid doesn't mean they aren't after you,' said some wise person. He would like to think she was too new at Cull to have developed loyalty for them so great that she would come after him. But that wasn't why she wouldn't do it. It was because she loved him like a father. He could feel it radiating off her. And he thought of her as the daughter he never had. And not just because she was smart, funny, and could kick butt like Jackie Chan.

So what was he feeling in his gut? Something? Nothing? He didn't know.

He would have to keep observing until all was well, just as he did every day with everyone wherever he was. But the thought of doing that made him ill.

He sipped his coffee, remembering two occasions when guys came on to her. One was a barista at Starbucks with purple streaks in his long hair and rings on his nose and lower lip. Ed had been standing behind Pearl. When he gave the guy whose behavior was out of line a look that had chilled the blood of many adversaries, the barista hurried into the back room.

About three months later, an older man sitting at a table near him and Pearl, interrupted Ed to ask her if she would like to hang out. The audacity and delusion of grandeur made them laugh at the guy. Pearl said, "No, thank you," and returned to talking with Ed. But still, the guy persisted. Ed told him that if he interrupted them again, he would squeeze his throat until his head turned purple like a big zit and popped all over his table. The unusual threat caused the guy to hyperventilate as he snatched his laptop and rushed out the door.

"Damn, Ed," Pearl said, "The poor guy nearly shit bricks." When they got up to leave, she slipped her arm through his and said, "Thanks, dad."

He had missed talking with her in person the past few months. They exchanged emails, texts, and phone calls, but their communication was always cryptic. While they used burner phones and emails with fake names, that wasn't enough for them to speak freely. And that was what he missed.

———

It was nearing 4 pm, and Ed was standing on his balcony looking out past the snow-covered lawn and heavy-ladened trees to the bus stop where Spruce Grove's walkway connected with the city's main sidewalk.

Moxie had been gone since 10:30, nearly six hours.

So where was she?

His relationship with Moxie was okay. For him, it wasn't a serious romance, but just two people who liked spending time together and spending time apart too. That was how he saw it, anyway. He got her the occasional gift… Actually, just one now that he thought about it. She was a gift giver—baked goods, socks, and a pen, stuff he didn't need. They had quality time together, sort of. Often, it led to arguments, though; two old timers stuck in their old ways. They weren't huggers. They had sex, which was fine but not great, but they didn't have intimate talks afterward. Or any other time, for that matter.

He enjoyed her company. She was smart and quick-witted; she understood him—what little he let her know about him—and they liked the same kind of films, mostly quiet, thought-provoking indie movies. One night Moxie brought her laptop to his apartment, saying she wanted them to watch a film one of the ladies in the canasta club suggested. She brought it up on her screen, and to Ed's surprise, it was a full-length porn movie, a good one. But when the heat of the moment cooled, everything was the same o'-same o'.

When he thought about it that way, it didn't sound like they had a heck of a lot going for them.

So why did Moxie start talking about marriage a few nights ago? That caught him off guard, and she didn't like his reaction.

So did he love her? He never thought about it until she started the marriage talk. If pressed, he would have to say that he wasn't sure. If forced to answer at gunpoint, he would have to say no. For sure, he didn't feel anything for her as he had for Florence, his late wife. He absolutely loved her, and he still did.

He took a ragged breath remembering the shock of her sudden death. How terrible it had been, and how lonely he had been since that devastating day.

Of all the women he'd known, only Florence knew what he did for a living. One day when he was feeling low about it, he remembered her saying, "You've helped your clients and how many others to be safe by eradicating undesirables so they may live more safely and without fear." Ed couldn't think of another woman who would have understood his work to the extent of saying something like that. And that included Moxie.

Apparently, Moxie loved him, as least enough to want to marry him. But did he want to marry her?

He took a deep breath and exhaled a long white stream into the cold air. No. He didn't want to marry her. What would be the point?

Ed shivered. It was 4:10 now, and it was getting even colder. What little daylight had struggled to get through the drab-gray, cloud-covered ceiling was dying.

Ed watched a city bus out on the street pass by the stop without slowing and continue northbound. Where was Moxie?

The skies began "spittin' snow," as Florence used to say, causing the automatic light poles along the walkway to flicker awake, but they didn't do much to fight off the gloom.

Ed tipped up one of the rattan chairs and tapped its front legs on the balcony floor to knock the soft snow off the seat. He plopped down on it, not caring if it made his butt wet, and stared past the railing to the expansive yard and snow-burdened spruce trees. A few branches had broken off and lay on the snow-covered ground like amputated arms and legs.

He didn't know how long he had been sitting there when he became aware of the fingers of both of his hands drumming on their respective armrests. His left hand abruptly stopped, but his right continued as if they had separate subconscious minds controlling them. A light wind blew some of the spittin' snow against his face, and his eyes blinked the irritation away as he watched his fingers and listened to their song.

Ed thought it was interesting that his thumb didn't participate other than waving slightly in the air as the four fingers on his right hand strummed the haunting beat. He asked himself why he found that interesting. He didn't know.

Or maybe he did. The fingers had found two spots on the rattan arm, about three inches apart, that produced two distinct sounds when tapped. The left one, a slight indent just before the armrest curved downward, made a "buh" sound. The one three inches to the right, its small indentation on the curve, made a heavier "bump" sound.

"Buh-bump…buh-bump…buh-bump…buh-bump…"

With his left hand, Ed felt his pulse on the side of his neck for a few seconds. It was in perfect synchronization with his drumming hand.

"'Here! It is the beating of his hideous heart,'" he said aloud to the frigid air, quoting Poe's "The Tell-Tale Heart."

He crossed his arms, tucking his numb fingers into his armpits. "I'm losing my mind," he whispered without humor.

He alerted on the sound of an accelerating city bus out on the street. He leaned forward to better see to the left through a break in the trees. A car passed, then another, their tires sounding wet on the yet-to-be-cleared asphalt. He could make out the bus's headlights, large and high off the street. Then the sound of its decelerating engine a second before it pulled to the curb in front of Spruce Grove's walkway. Moxie had to be on it.

He would wolf whistle at her like a construction worker, and she would wave him off as usual or flip him the finger if she was in a feisty mood.

He smiled. Maybe he didn't love Mox, but he liked her. Some say that's just as important, maybe more so. They had some nice times, and she was good company. She knew when he wanted to be alone for a couple of days, and he could cheer her up when she needed it. That kind of intuition about each other—

The bus accelerated away. She didn't get off.

A heavyset black woman named Rose Monroe did, or as she often sang in an exaggerated southern accent when she flirted with Ed, "I'm Rosie, a whole lotta lovin', Mon-roe." The custodian hadn't swept the snow off the walkway yet, so she had to step carefully. Old people, snow, and falling were not a good mix. She saw him watching her and waved.

"Mox wasn't on the bus with you, Rosie?" Ed rhetorically called down to her when she was close enough to hear.

She shielded her eyes against the wind-blown snow as she looked up at him. "No. I ran into her at Barnes and Noble at about one thirty or so. We chatted briefly, then we went in separate directions."

"She say where she was off to?"

Rose thought for a minute, then shook her head. "No, I guess she didn't. Oh, wait. Yes, sorry. She said she was going to Ellen's to get some heavier gloves. Said this damned cold weather hurts her fingers something awful." She shook her head. "I'm not that brave to wander that far down toward the river. Beautiful store, but the street scum is settin' up their camps closer and closer to that area."

"Yeah, this weather bothers her fingers and toes a lot." He thanked Rose and headed inside to dig out a small spiral notebook that Moxie had made for him. She had written "Fone Numbuhs" on it, deliberately misspelling the two words. It was her kind of humor. He looked up Toni's number, one of the women at the breakfast table this morning.

"It's Ed, Toni," he said loudly to the partially deaf 94-year-old.

"You gonna come over, handsome?"

"Someday, I'll take you up on that, pretty lady." He could practically smell the rose-scented powder she so liberally sprinkled all over herself. "Listen, I wanted to ask you if Moxie said anything about going somewhere today."

"Let me think… Yes. Yes, she did."

"I see. Did she say where, Toni?"

"Shopping. I just said that. You're getting' old, mister."

Ed fake-laughed, then, "Was it downtown, Toni? She's been gone much longer than her usual, and it's terribly cold outside."

"She was gonna go downtown to that big department store. Uh, oh yes, Meier and Frank. Wait, they changed their name to…"

"They changed it to Macy's, Toni. But they closed that one in twenty-sixteen, I think. She shops at Ellen's now, anyway."

"That's what I said, Ed. Jesus!" She hung up on him.

He looked out the sliding glass door. It was dark now. The outdoor lights normally created an enchanted winter wonderland feel when snowing, but not this time. Now it was more…foreboding.

"What the hell," he said aloud. Then thought, I just described the dark out the window as foreboding. And after all that I've been through over the years.

He was tired from being awakened by his imaginary visitor the night before, but he needed to find Moxie. There was a 5:45 bus that went downtown. The busses so far this afternoon had been on time, which meant the city hadn't changed to snow routes. At least not yet.

He headed for his closet to retrieve his heavier coat, an ash-colored Canadian Goose Expedition Parka that he picked up in New York City three years back for $1700.00. It was worth it. Packed with 625-fill down made it wind and water-resistant and kept him toasty warm.

An excellent coat to ward off the snow, the dark, and the foreboding.

Chapter 6

Ed's first thought when he awoke was that he was lying in a deep grave filled with snow. His upper body was warm, but his bare face and hands felt at once numb and achy. His eyes wanted more sleep, but he instinctively knew he shouldn't and tried to force them open. But he managed only a slit, feeling scratchy pain in his orbs and seeing only whiteness. He gave up and closed them. Are my eyes frozen shut?

Have I fallen? He had gone down in the backyard about three weeks ago. It wasn't a dizzy spell, but down he went, dropping to his knees first, then onto his face. He got back up, no worse for the wear, but it startled him a little. Have I done it again?

The pain, like dozens of icicles no larger than a pinpoint, stabbed and scraped his eyeball as he forced his left eye open. Damn, that hurt. Then he strained to open his right; that one was agonizing.

Deep grave? Ice cycles poking my eyes? What the hell?

He pushed himself onto his elbow, blinking the rest of the ice away from his eyes. It was night; when did that happen? He squinted at his blurry surroundings: snow all around him, ghostly trees drooping from the weight of their white burden. Hazy circles of light on the snow-covered ground below the light poles did little to illuminate the frozen, colorlessness yard.

Clarity returned to his vision, revealing a lead-colored, low-hanging ceiling dumping more snow on him and the surroundings. Are those my legs? he wondered, not feeling them. They must be, and they got about a quarter inch of snow on them.

He sat up and quickly plunged his stiff, frozen hands into his fur-lined coat pockets as his mind began to clear along with his eyes. He was sitting on a blanket of snow about 30 yards from Spruce Grove. Visibility around the dark grounds was helped a little by the walkway lights and the Grove's six floors of well-lit balconies. He located his apartment on the top floor, the bottom two-thirds of his sliding glass door hidden behind the railing.

Someone had used a push broom to move snow from the walkway but apparently had given up after about 10 feet from the front doors. Halfway to the street, partially filled footprints led across the snow-covered lawn to where he lay. He frowned. Why did I leave the walkway? And why am I out here, anyway?

"I have to get up," he said to himself, but it was easier said than done with every joint stiff with cold.

"Made it," he said after a struggle. He waited until he stopped swaying before brushing off his Goose Expedition parka. He was happy to be wearing it but wished he had thought to bring his gloves and a hat.

Hell, he couldn't even remember getting dressed, coming out here, and why it came to be that he was sleeping in the snow. Then he did.

I was going to catch the bus downtown and look for Moxie, he thought, feeling better that some memory had returned. He looked at his footprints again. Why would I make a 90-degree right turn off the sidewalk and walk out here? He looked down at the flattened snow. I must have slipped and fallen. Did I hit my head? It doesn't hurt, other than I have a brain freeze.

He pulled his hands out of the coat's warmth and trudged toward the sidewalk, his arms waving like a tightrope walker.

"You finally woke up, you bastard!"

Ed stopped, recognizing the crackly, obnoxious voice of his nemesis, Ben, an asshole through and through. Ed found the third floor and the geezer's balcony, where he had shouted down at Ed numerous other times. Ben, 92, had fought at Omaha Beach in World War II and with the First Marines in the Korean War. At least, that's what he claims. Ed needed to learn more about the two battles to ask him a trick question or two.

Ben shouted again, his gravelly voice full of delight. "This is nothing, Ed. When I was in Korea, we would piss in our pants to keep us warm."

"You still do, Ben, and worse."

Ben leaned so far over his railing, sending snow from the railing down to the ground, that Ed thought he might sail out into space. The old man shook his fist. "Anytime, you bastard," Ben shouted. "Any Goddamn time." Ed smiled up at him and commenced trudging stiffly toward the walkway. "By the way," Ben shouted, not letting the moment go, "I thought about telling the front desk you passed out and fell down in the snow, but that wouldn't have been as much fun as watching you lay there for twenty minutes, freezing your nuts off. You son-of-a-bitch!"

Ed commenced trudging, not remembering why Ben disliked him so. When he didn't hear anything further from him, he glanced up to his third-floor balcony. He saw the head and shoulders of a woman behind him, her movements indicating she was pulling Ben's wheelchair back through his sliding glass door. Her name was Theresa, the cranky man's 60-year-old daughter. He returned her wave, remembering their torrid weekend at Snowfall Motel up at Mt. Hood before he met Florence. Theresa mentioned a few weeks later when he had bumped into her at the front door entrance, that she had let it slip to her father that they had spent the weekend together.

Ah, that's why Ben hates me, Ed remembered. It was worth it, though.

He reached the snow-covered walkway without falling. Frowning, he looked back at where he had awakened. He tenderly touched his head, front and back, and shrugged his shoulders to see if he had jammed an arm. Nothing hurt.

He hadn't heard a passing vehicle out on the street or any other sound since Ben had gone in. Not a breeze altered the falling flakes from their silent, vertical descent. With their heavy, white shrouds, the spruce evergreens stood still, helpless to the accumulating weight on their drooping extremities.

Ed glanced toward the street, some 20 yards away, the snow undisturbed.

But someone was sitting on a wooden bench that encircled the trunk of one the largest trees near the city sidewalk. There was enough pale light from the closest light pole to reveal a man, white, in his mid-40s, dressed inexplicably in a colorful Hawaiian shirt and tan shorts.

Slowly, robotically, his head swiveled toward Ed.

Ed staggered slightly, a faint whine coming from somewhere deep in his chest.

The man stood, his long arms hanging limply along his sides, his face without expression, though Ed could feel his eyes, the dead in them. And something else.

Accusation.

Ed's heart pounded in his throat.

The man turned stiffly back toward the tree as if his joints had turned to ice in the deep cold. He stepped toward the large trunk like a man with frozen knees walking on thin ice. Before he disappeared behind it, he turned his stiff neck just enough to look at Ed once more and kept looking until he was out of sight behind the tree.

The tree trunk was broad but not enough to hide a colorful flash of the ridiculous Hawaiian shirt on its right side, then on the left.

Ed feared that his hammering heart might burst from his chest. Not because he saw the man, but rather what seeing him meant.

The man wasn't there.

He couldn't be.

Ed had killed him on a hot summer day years ago.

Simon Glass, Ed remembered. A performer, specifically a Shakespearian actor, who enjoyed fame in Chicago's theater world. Ed's orders from The Organization were to terminate him with a bodkin, a long needle mentioned by Hamlet in his famous soliloquy about taking his own life.

Ed did as ordered by inserting the bodkin numerous times into the man's carotid arteries on both sides of his neck. One side would have killed the man, but as requested, Ed speared both three times. He knew that pulling the bodkin out after each plunge would affect the greatest blood geysers. Ed checked the target's pulse during the 20 minutes he was on the scene, though the shrinking blood arcs from the sides of his neck and fast-expanding pool around his head made his demise quite apparent.

As with the majority of his 70-plus hits, Ed didn't ask why the man was to be terminated, but he assumed it had something to do with the papers he was told to take with him when he left the scene.

That hit had been many years ago, and Ed had nearly forgotten it, but after "seeing" the actor, the details came flooding back. He shoved his bare hands into his fur-lined coat pockets—his right hand feeling the $10 Jiffi Box Cutter—and walked slowly toward the tree. His old heart hammered, and his struggling breathing emitted frosty white puffs around his head.

The large Spruce sheltered the bench from the falling snow. The wet dirt in front of it revealed only squirrel tracks, as did the snow that haloed the trunk five feet out from it. No one, that is, no one *alive,* had stepped here. Still, Ed cautiously circled the tree, the cutter in his hand hovering at the ready a few inches out from his chest.

No one was there, and the snow on that side was untouched.

Ed closed his eyes and sucked in his breath. I'm finally going crazy, he thought, and it's about damn time. A car slowly passed on the street, a loose chain on one of the tires banging against something. He didn't open his eyes. Instead, he focused on counting his breaths: in, out slowly; in, out slowly...

He opened them. The north and south lanes showed only a few tire tracks; Portlanders weren't used to the snow and stayed home when possible. Flakes fell lazily all about the large spruce trees near the street. Ed looked at the trunks of each, clear. What about the trees behind him, he thought, his heart thumping in his chest. Fear.

Not a word he uses when applied to himself.

He forced himself to turn about to look at the many other Spruce trees between him and the Home. He sucked in his breath...

Twenty feet to his left, a man stood beside a tree trunk, white T-shirt blood-soaked, his palms extended toward Ed as if to hold him back.

Ed remembered the man and knew he couldn't be real. He turned his head away from the sight, but 30 feet away to his left, another tree and another man, this one sitting with his back against the trunk, legs sprawled in front of him. The side of his head was indented and dripping red. Lying next to him was a large, vintage sledgehammer with mushroom ends, used decades ago by railroad track layers to hammer down spikes. Ed remembered him, too, a retired train conductor and collector of railroad memorabilia. And kiddie porn he photographed himself.

Directly ahead of him were two medium-sized trees, a man next to each trunk. One was spasming on the ground, his thrashing feet kicking snow all about. The other was smoking, with one foot braced behind him against the tree, rope burns around his neck visible even from 40 feet away.

Ed walked toward the walkway as quickly as his cold joints and the slippery ground allowed. Halfway there, he tried to run but nearly fell twice before he forced himself to slow. Ed saw movement out of the corners of his eyes, twice to his left, where there were two trees, and once to his right by the oldest Spruce. Ed refused to look.

He pushed through the double glass doors, crossed the small vestibule, and pushed through the next set of doors. No one was sitting in the lobby sofas at this hour, so he plopped down in the closest one, shut his eyes, and focused on slowing his rapid heart rate. Two minutes passed.

"Oh, hi, Ed."

He snapped open his eyes, feeling his pulse streak back up to 180, more likely 200.

"Sylvia," he managed to the night desk person.

"You look awful, Ed. Are you okay? Why were you out in the snow?"

"I'm…I'm fine." He stood with a couple of grunts. "I was, uh, making a snowman." He pointed at the sofa. "Thought I'd sit for a second before going up."

Sylvia frowned slightly, not getting the joke or understanding why he would want to sit down here. "I see. Oh, by the way, someone called asking about you."

"Who, what, and when, Sylvia?"

"That's a funny way to ask, Ed. Who: He didn't say who he was, but he sounded youngish. You know, twenty, I think. What: He wanted to know if you were in. I told him I'd transfer him to you because, you know, I don't give out too much information about people here. Lots of scammers, you know. And when? About, uh, 90 minutes ago, give or take."

He nodded. "Thank you. Good night, Sylvia." He headed toward the elevator but stopped before he got there. "Oh, Sylvia. Have you seen Mox? Did she come in?"

She shook her head. "I haven't. But I assume she's tucked in, all warm and cozy at this hour."

Ed hesitated at Moxie's door on the sixth floor, unsure about knocking. He finally did, but with just a light tap, his ear pressed against the door. Nothing. "Mox?" he whispered loudly. At the risk of pissing her off even more, he inserted his key, opened it a crack, and called her name into the darkness.

Silence.

"I'm coming in, Mox," he said. "Hit me with a skillet if you want, but I have to know you're home." Silence. Her balcony lights were on, but they always were, 24/7, using them when she slept as a nightlight. Ed slipped past her kitchen counter and saw her bed empty and still made from this morning.

The Model A car horn sounded from his pants pocket, three times as loud in the silence of Mox's apartment. Ed quickly retrieved it. The screen read Front Counter.

"They call again, Sylvia?" He quick-peeked into Moxie's closet. Three empty hangers.

"What? Oh, no, no, not a call. But someone brought a package for you."

"Package?"

"About as big as a shoebox. It just says 'Ed' and 'Spruce Grove' under that. No address. Early Christmas present?"

He closed Moxie's door behind him. "Beats me. I'll be down in a moment. Thanks."

He poked the elevator button and stood by the window where hours earlier he had watched the rooster known as Chick Norris stab a rat to death with its dagger-like spurs, then look up at him. He could barely make out the chicken pen in the dark at this hour. He called Toni again.

"I just told you five minutes ago she went to Meier and Franks," Toni snapped after Ed apologized for the late call, then asked again if she had heard from Moxie.

"Sorry, Toni. It's just that—"

"You've called me a dozen times, and the answer is still no. I'm going to tell Charlie you're harassing me."

"Charlie's the custodian, Toni," Ed said. "Have a good night."

He ignored the elevators doors opening and headed back to his room to get out of his overcoat. He would have to take it to the cleaners and get it tidied up after "sleeping" in the snow. He hung it up in his bathroom, then headed back out the door.

"What a strange day," he said aloud as he descended to the lobby. "I watched a rooster and rat fight, had a squabble with Mox, didn't enjoy a nap in the snow, and saw many people I haven't seen since I terminated them." He shook his head. "And now I'm talking to myself."

The elevator dinged, and the doors swooshed open. Sylvia had reduced the number of lit lights in the entry area and cafeteria as per this hour's routine. Normally, Ed wouldn't have given the semi-darkness a thought, but after a day of hallucinations...

He peered into the dining room, where a single wall light across the large room kept the place from total darkness. Ed could see the neatly arranged tables and chairs and the precisely centered salt and pepper shakers in the dimness. The hall would be packed in the morning with folks gossiping and telling of old experiences.

Ed looked away before his mind filled the chairs with those he had sent to the cloaked reaper with the large scythe.

Sylvia stepped out of the office door. "There you are, Ed. I thought I heard the elevator ding." She walked toward him, the 'shoebox-sized' package leading the way. "It's been wrapped in grocery store bag paper, no stamps or return address. Really light. Maybe it's a gift card." She looked at him, expecting an explanation.

"Any idea who brought it?" he asked, taking the box.

"Sure. The delivery person rang the front door buzzer. Startled the bejesus out of me. It was a young man in his twenties. No one comes to the door this late, plus the shitty weather out there. Whoops. Sorry," she said, lifting her palm in front of her mouth. "I've been trying to watch my language."

"You said the caller sounded like he was in his twenties. Was it the same voice as the delivery person?"

"I think so."

"What did he look like?"

"Kind of like a really cold street person, shivering. He was dressed shabby, wearing a wet coat that wasn't helping much out in the snow. He had long red hair. I mean really red, dyed maybe, an unshaven face, pimply forehead. Bad teeth too. He looked like those people in a *Time* magazine article about meth addiction. He gave me the creeps the way he kept looking over my shoulder into the place. Like he was going to bowl over me to get in. It might have been my imagination. It gets a little spooky down here on the night shift sometimes. Come down and keep me company if you can't sleep."

"Thanks for calling me. The front door secure again?"

She nodded. "I peeked through the office blinds and watched the young man trudge back to the street, turn left, and disappear. I'd feel sorry for him if he didn't give me the heebie-jeebies so much."

Ed walked over to the door and checked it anyway. He cupped his eyes to block the light reflection from the lobby, noting fresh prints in the snow coming and going. He turned back to Sylvia. "Call me if anything makes you uncomfortable, okay? Charlie's working tonight, right?"

"He's mopping the kitchen."

Ed examined all sides of the feather-weight box in the elevator. Nearly every inch of it was taped heavily with two-inch wide clear tape. He would need his boxcutter to open it, which, he remembered, he had left in his overcoat. The doors slid open to an empty, quiet hallway. He eyed Mox's door as he headed down the hall.

Inside his apartment, he placed the box on the kitchen counter and retrieved a knife. He glanced at the sliding glass door to his balcony, not expecting anyone to be peering in again, but glad there wasn't. He had had enough visitors for one day.

He sawed at the tape. It wasn't uncommon for him to get packages, usually left outside his door—brownies, freshly baked bread, a nice cabernet sauvignon. All of them were delivered in-house, some anonymous, most with a note and name. But this was the first one to be brought to Spruce Grove's front door by a messenger, let alone in bad weather at this late hour.

He cut off enough tape to open the four flaps, exposing wads of tissue. Ed picked up a pen and poked the paper aside enough to reveal a plastic bag, like those found in a grocery produce area. Something was inside, but he couldn't see what it was. He slid the box directly under the counter light and bent down to see—

Ed snapped his head back and quick-stepped away as if avoiding a punch.

He stood frozen, looking at the box's open flaps, his chest heaving as if he had just jogged up the six floors to his room. He collected himself enough to inch forward, slowly as if approaching a deadly snake.

The tissue he had pushed to one end came into view, then the produce bag, its end tied off with a green paper twist tie like supermarkets use. The tissue was to keep the contents from rolling around so that when he opened the flaps, naturally from the top, the presentation would have its greatest effect.

Ed could see about an inch of the thing in the bag, enough to know that it was a human finger, the nail painted purple. "What the...?"

He used his pen again to push the tissue aside further to see the rest of— "No!"

A surge of nausea and trepidation washed over his body, intensifying as he stared with disbelief into the box.

The finger wore a ring, a walnut-sized amethyst purple stone. Moxie told him once that it cost her a little under a thousand dollars because of all the extras the jeweler had designed into it.

Chapter 7

Ed had no idea what he was wearing other than a full-length coat with a fur-lined hoodie, gloves, and warm boots. A wind had picked up, rustling the great trees in Spruce Grove's front yard, blowing the snow off their boughs and into his face and body, along with the fresh stuff falling from the sky. The cold air burned his nose and watered his eyes, but he paid it no mind.

He had slipped past Sylvia in the front office to exit the home from the north door, knowing she never watched the side door cameras. Moving from deep shadow to deep shadow, he made his way across the yard, now covered with about five inches of snow, through the trees that earlier had been visited by entities he had terminated. Reaching the sidewalk, he trudged southbound, his body bent into the frigid wind, well out of sight of anyone looking out their apartment window. He hadn't seen a single vehicle pass at the late hour. One of the few bus-stop shelters not vandalized in the city offered Ed some reprieve from the wind gusts, strong enough now to make him stagger.

A dozen thoughts bounced around in Ed's skull. How did the abductors know who he was, where he lived, and his relationship with Mox? Or was it even about that? Maybe it was a stretch to assume they knew who he was and what he had done for so many years. If they did know, which he was leaning toward believing, they no doubt figured he wouldn't notify the Portland Police or the FBI because their investigation might lead them to the existence of The Organization in Australia and Cull, Liam White's group.

He peeked around the edge of his hoodie at the sound of a vehicle's approach. A truck, big, white, without chains. It slowed a quarter of a block away and then stopped in the lane next to the bus stop. The passenger door swung open, revealing Pearl stretched across the seat from the driver's side. "Hop in, Ed. I got the heater blazing for you."

"Good idea not calling the police," she said as Ed settled into the big seat and fastened his seatbelt. He pulled off his gloves and rubbed his palms together in front of the blowing heat vent. She was wearing her gloves, which Ed knew trainees were instructed to do in their training. "Leave no prints" was the often-repeated refrain in the business. This included private vehicles.

"After you called, I cruised up Seventh on the way here to see what kind of activity was happening at the homeless camp on Apple Street. Most of the tents were dark at this hour, but there were a few lit from inside." She turned the big truck around in a driveway and headed back in the direction she had come, all the while talking. "I saw a couple of barrel fires with people standing around them. If this red-haired kid walked to your place, that camp is only six blocks away. The bus stopped service at 11 p.m., so according to when your office called you, he could have taken it to deliver the package, but he would have had to walk back."

She looked at Ed. "You haven't said anything."

"You haven't given me a chance."

"Sorry, Ed. I'm just freaked a little." She touched his forearm, then returned her hand to the wheel. "How are you doing? That must have been awful opening that package." She stopped at a red light. "On the phone, you said we should check the homeless camps and shelters for the delivery guy. Is the one on Apple Street a good place to start?"

"Yes."

Ed's monkey brain bounced from the image of the neatly severed finger, to the dead man on his balcony, to the rooster looking up for his reaction to its kill, to looking at Moxie's ring at breakfast, to the dead man in the Hawaiian shirt disappearing behind the tree, to the strained conversation he and Mox had about marriage to—

"I'm glad I was in town to be with you."

Ed blinked himself back to the moment. "Yes. I appreciate your coming out in the storm to help me. And volunteering your truck, too."

She reached for his forearm again, squeezing it gently this time. "I would have been upset if you hadn't called." When he said nothing, Pearl lifted her thumb off the steering wheel. "You said on the phone that your front desk woman told you that the red-haired guy was shabbily dressed, his hair looked dyed, his face covered with pimples, and he had bad teeth. She thought he looked like a meth addict. I leave anything out?"

"He didn't cross the street to the southbound bus stop. Instead, he turned south on the closest sidewalk to Spruce Grove and walked until he disappeared from her line of sight."

"That means he walked there. Or maybe someone drove him there, dropped him off a short distance away, he walked up to Spruce Grove and delivered the package, then walked back to catch his ride."

Ed shrugged. "Anything is possible, except Sylvia said he was wet and shivering."

"In that case, he probably walked both ways." Pearl pointed at the windshield. "My money is on this place." She pulled a quarter block short of the camp that began at the curb and extended into a lot.

Ed scanned the site to get a quick read from where they were idling. The building on this side of the lot appeared empty; the one on the other side, he couldn't tell. The lot was large, jammed width and depth with tents and makeshift shelters of every configuration. He saw a barrel fire with half a dozen people huddled around it, some wearing shabby coats and others with blankets wrapped around them. They were passing a large jug of wine back and forth and didn't appear to be talking.

"I watched a documentary on the homeless," Pearl said, eyeing the camp as carefully as Ed. "Most of them have a boss or captain who takes care of conflicts and such. I would think their camp would be near the entrance." She looked at Ed. "How do you want to do it?"

"Let's see if we can find your camp captain."

They climbed out of the Dodge Ram and walked to its front. "Okay, here we go," Pearl said, eyeing the woman moving toward them. Ed had already noticed her; middle-aged, thin, with bird-like sharp features, frazzled graying hair, wearing greasy blue jeans and a tattered blue parka. She gripped a wooden baseball bat in both hands, the overhead streetlight sparkling off the nails protruding from the bat's fat end.

"Hey, what you want here, you two?" The accented voice was hoarse, tired. "See the bat, right, you two? Ain't no missin' it, right? Fuck wit me or fuck wit my people, I put holes in yer skulls, right?" The woman had a lump under one side of her bottom lip. A small trail of brown chewing tobacco curled down her chin.

Ed and Pearl stayed where they were. Pearl spoke first. "You must be head of the camp, ma'am."

"Got that correct, Barbie, you do." She eyed Ed, her mouth working the chew. "You wantin' to donate, why you doin' it the middle of the night?"

"We're looking for a young man," Ed said.

"He speaks, he does. You wantin' a young man for your own perverted old self, or for this here pretty one?" Pearl gave the woman a you-got-to-be-kidding look. "Yuh dissin me now wit that look, are yuh now,

Barbie?" the woman snapped. She took a step forward, her eyes on Pearl, her hands adjusting on the bat, gripping it like she was about to swing it. "There's blood under that snow where you're standin', you two. That came from an asshole who dissed me last night, 'bout this same time. Yuh come here to laugh at me and my people—"

"Didn't mean any disrespect, ma'am," Ed said quickly, stepping slightly in front of Pearl, who looked like she was ready to do some bitch slapping. "We're looking for a red-haired man, 20s, to give him a tip for doing a little work for me earlier this evening. We don't know his name." Pearl moved around from behind Ed, shooting him an annoyed look.

"What kinda work he do?" the woman asked, wiping the back of her hand across her running nose. She looked at it after, then glared at Pearl.

"Made a delivery," Ed said. "You got a young man who looks like that? His hair is bright red and long."

"Cost yuh twenty." The woman's eyes scanned Ed up and down. She sniffed, wiped her tearing eyes with the heel of her hand, then swiped her nose again. "Sumptin' 'bout you ain't right. I can't see it, but I can feel it on you."

Ed pulled a twenty-dollar bill from his wallet. "I'm stepping closer, okay?" he said, looking at her bat.

The woman nodded slightly and extended her hand, her eyes not leaving his. Ed passed the money to her without getting beaned. She looked at it, then stuffed it into her back pocket. "He's got a lean-to, all tarps and boards propped against that far building. It's 'bout forty feet back from the sidewalk. It's the only one like that over there."

"What's his name?" Ed asked.

"Wouldn't yuh know that already?" the woman asked suspiciously. Ed shrugged. She eyed him a moment longer. "Everyone calls him 'Strawberry.' Ain't too bright. Fact is, he ain't bright at all. But that don't mean you can fuck with him."

Ed shook his head. "No intention to do anything like that, ma'am. Thank you." He and Pearl started to move in the direction of the building.

"Hold up, Barbie," the woman said to Pearl. "You stay here with me. Don't take two of yuh tuh give him some money." Pearl opened her mouth to say something. "That's the way it's gonna be. Otherwise, neither of yuh goin' back, and I keep the twenty."

"I got it," Ed said to Pearl. "I won't be long."

"But—"

"I got this," he said firmly, then turned to make his way toward the building.

He navigated around all the garbage and human waste on the sidewalk to where the four-story building bordered one side of the encampment. Except for a few tents here and there where their interior lights dimly lit their exteriors, much of the camp was in near darkness. He could hear snores nearby and the sound of thin traffic on the I-5 freeway about four blocks away.

Ed's cellphone flashlight helped a little as he worked his way around tents, more garbage, cooking setups, more feces, boxes, bottles, and a pile of something he didn't recognize, but it stunk like a decaying animal. He heard lovemaking from a dirty-white teepee, and from a yellow teepee next to it, a gravelly voice threatened to drive an axe into Ed's face if he tried to steal something.

The boy's lean-to was as described: broken pieces of wood hammered together to form a frame with scraps of canvas, blankets, and cardboard. The weight of the snow had collapsed one of its corners.

"Strawberry?" Ed said softly. "Strawberry. Wake up, please." He heard stirring within. "Strawberry?"

"Just a sec; Holy smokes, what time is it?"

Ed sidestepped to the collapsed end should he come out swinging punches.

The young man's head poked out of the small opening first; the redness of his hair wasn't overstated. Then like a dog cautiously exiting a kennel, his shoulders emerged, his upper torso, and finally, his legs. He moved on his all-fours until he had completely cleared the tent and could stand. His eyes looked sleepy in Ed's cellphone light.

"You're too old to be a cop."

"Too smart too. You awake?"

"Yeah. Why'd you wake me up? I was dreaming about my doggy, King. He used to sleep with me when I was six...no, eight. He—"

"You brought a package to me two hours ago at Spruce Grove. I'm Ed."

Strawberry's eyes widened comically, then spun around and dashed off toward the sidewalk, jumping over piles of whatever. "Strawberry! Stop! You're not in trouble. I just—"

"Aaaagh!" the boy cried out as his shin struck something, sending him sprawling on top of a small tent. "Hey, asshole!" a voice growled, sounding like it came from inside the tent the boy fell into. "I'm going to kick your ass!" Strawberry righted himself and took off again.

Ed took a step to pursue, but his foot caught on something. He managed to keep his balance with a lot of arm waving as he shouted, "Pearl! He's coming out on the sidewalk! Stop him!"

"Hey, get back here, bitch! You hearin' me?" screeched the camp boss.

"Whereabouts, Ed?"

"Right where that first blue tent is!"

Ed came around a tall black teepee just as Strawberry and Pearl met by the blue tent. Pearl greeted him with a fast round kick that slammed into the young man's right side. Liver hit, Ed noted. Always a showstopper.

Pearl grabbed a wad of his jacket and guided his collapsing body down onto the sidewalk to protect his head from impacting the cement. Ed had seen her make that Good Samaritan gesture one other time after she had sent a poor sap head-first toward the concrete. Ed stopped next to the writhing redhead.

"Breathe," Pearl said, taking a knee beside the boy. "Be glad I didn't hit you with all my power."

"Why'd...you...kick...me?" Strawberry managed between moans and gasps.

"Why did you run?" Ed asked before snapping his head to his left.

"Stop right there!" he blared, stepping between Pearl and the camp captain about to swing a homerun blow to the back of her head. He jammed the woman's hands and bat against her chest and pushed her back. "We're on a public sidewalk, so this has nothing to do with you. And you just tried to hit a woman with a deadly weapon. Back off, or we're pressing charges with the police."

The woman retreated two steps, her eyes blazing. "Yuh okay, Strawberry?" she called out.

"Think so."

"We just want to talk to you," Pearl said to the boy, pulling gently on his upper arm. "That's all."

Strawberry moaned as he struggled to sit up. He looked down at his side as if to see through his clothes at his nauseatingly painful liver.

"Privately," Ed told the woman. He pointed in the direction of Strawberry's lean-to. "Or we call nine-one-one to report those people back there cooking heroin in a spoon and what you were about to do with your bat."

"Where?" the woman snapped, squinting into the darkness. She stormed off in the direction of Ed's lie.

"Let's get him up onto his feet," Ed said, taking the young man's other arm. He looked down the sidewalk. "There's a lighted inset to this building down there," he said, indicating an entrance about 50 feet away.

Halfway to the inset, Strawberry was walking fine, but they kept hold of his arms anyway. "You like this snow, son?" Ed asked.

"Used to when I was little. But it's just cold now, and I get sick a lot."

"Sorry to hear," Ed said. "Who gave you the box?"

"Crazy Dumpy."

Ed and Pearl guided Strawberry into the inset. It was no warmer, but at least the snow wasn't falling on them. "Who's that?"

Strawberry looked at Ed. "You don't know him? Everybody does. I ain't jokin' when I say he's crazy as a bedbug." He chuckled and shook his head. "That's what my friend Tommy always says. Like bedbugs are supposed to be crazy or somethin'."

"Where is he?"

"Tommy? I think—"

"No, this guy, Dumpy."

"Oh. Sorry. I'm kinda slow, you know. My mama told me I was sick or somethin' when I was a baby and didn't get enough air, so my brain got somethin' wrong with it, kinda."

"Sorry to hear, Strawberry," Ed said. "You seem fine to me." The young man smiled wide at that. "Where is this crazy as a bedbug guy?"

Strawberry laughed hard at that, the sound like a donkey's bray. When he stopped, he said, "He owns the used clothes store. Lives in the back."

"Which one? There are lots of them around here."

"Dumpy's. It's on the window."

"By the Salvation Army?" Pearl asked.

Strawberry nodded vigorously. "Yeah, yeah, yeah."

"I know where it is," Pearl told Ed.

"How did he come to give it to you?" Ed asked. "The box, I mean."

"I go there a lot, see, so he knows me. One time, I didn't have enough money for what I wanted, but he let me take some clothes if I promised to bring him the rest. I got enough panhandling that day and brought him the money before he closed. So he knows I'm honest, you know."

"A fine trait, son. Did he tell you what was in the box?"

Strawberry shook his head. "I thought it was weed or somethin' 'cause it was so light. Thought maybe you was the dope cops."

"It was a finger." Ed watched for his reaction.

"Wadda you mean…finger?" Ed wiggled his in front of Strawberry's face. The young man screwed up his face. "For reals? But Dumpy had all his today when I seen him there."

"You think he's in his living space in the back right now?"

Strawberry shrugged. "Probably. I don't think he drinks or nothin'. I know he has a TV 'cause you can kinda see it back there from out in his store." He thought for a moment, then shook his head vigorously. "Like a finger? A person's finger, right?"

Chapter 8

Ed and Pearl were back in the truck, enjoying the heat blowing on them. "You're a softy, Ed. You gave Strawberry enough money to stay at the Marriott."

Ed shrugged. "I've been thinking that whoever has Mox is connected in some way to one of my jobs. But unless Strawberry was lying to us, this Dumpy character might change that theory."

"But what else would be the possible motive?"

Ed shook his head.

"Poor Moxie," Pearl said, looking at him compassionately. "A finger. Jesus H! I mean, are you okay, Ed?"

He looked out the side window without answering. He didn't understand what his thoughts, or lack of them, meant regarding Mox's abduction. If the finger amputation had happened to Florence, he would have gone berserk, mowing down anyone in his way.

Ed did feel guilty thinking about why she was abducted, that it might have been because of him and one of his past jobs. But the guilty feeling was the same intensity he would experience if someone else at Spruce Grove, like Charlie, Bill, Sylvia, or even cranky Ben, had been abducted and hurt because of him.

"There's the place right there on the corner," Pearl said, nodding at the windshield.

Ed had passed through this part of Portland a few times. It wasn't in skid row, but it was close and was more and more looking like the row: potholed streets, garbage-strewn sidewalks, junked cars, and clusters of tents here and there.

They circled the block, noting that there wasn't an alleyway behind the building that housed Dumpy's little shop. Pearl parked in a No Parking zone two doors down from the dingy door with DUMPY'S scrawled in white paint across the dark front window.

"How do you want to play it?" Pearl asked, looking out the windshield. "Snow's keeping people off the street, so that's good."

"You stand off to the side of the door out of sight. I'll knock and pretend to need something for the cold. He looked at the backseat. Let me use that blanket."

Ed removed his overcoat without removing his gloves and wrapped the gray blanket around his shoulders. "Perfect," Pearl said, pushing a finger between each of hers to remove the slack out of her gloves. They got out of the truck, squinting from a snow gust smacking their faces. "I'll wait a minute until I follow you."

In Dumpy's doorway, Ed scanned both sides of the street to ensure no passersby. He put his face near the front door window, which had never seen a spray of Windex or a swipe of a paper towel, noting a semi-dark room cluttered with wooden bins piled with clothing. The walls were covered with more clothing on hangers hooked over large nails. A dim light came from a half-opened door at the back of the room. The man's living quarters, Ed remembered Strawberry saying.

He pounded on the door facing, then on the door's glass. He looked over at Pearl, standing just out of sight of anyone looking out the main window or the one in the door. He pounded harder. A shadow passed by the light coming from the door in the back. A moment later, a large silhouette passed through the doorway and moved into the dark store.

"Closed!" a voice bellowed, sounding as if it were coming from a tuba. "It's midnight."

"I got money, sir. Lots of it. Me and my wife and kid are freezing. It won't take long; I need to get clothes for all of us. We got ripped off tonight."

"Hold on," the tuba voice said irritably. "You got ten minutes, then I throw your ass out the door."

"Thank you, sir," Ed said through the glass. He watched the man's dark form lumber over to a desk at the side of the room and pick up a key. "Thank you so much, sir," Ed called to him.

"You got me believing you," Pearl whispered.

When Dumpy turned back to the door, the light bar from the back room hit him just enough to reveal that he was wearing only white boxers and a tattered, unzipped sweatshirt; his enormous belly led the way. The thought of this man touching Moxie charged Ed's blood with adrenaline. The man unlocked three door locks.

"You're lucky I wasn't asleep yet," Dumpy said, opening the door. "Lemme see your cash first, pal." Ed shrugged the blanket off his shoulders but didn't move to retrieve his wallet. The fat man's pig eyes moved to his face. "Hey, you're too fuckin' old to have a kid—" His eyes widened fearfully as Pearl pealed around the inset. "What the hell is thi—"

Ed slapped his palm over the man's eyes.

Dumpy's natural reflex snapped his head back, which shifted his profound poundage back onto his heels, making it easy for Pearl, with both her hands and Ed with his remaining one, to shove his largeness back into the room until his rhino-sized butt bumped up against a clothing bin. Pearl back-kicked the door shut without removing her hands from his chest.

Ed withdrew his hands and stepped back enough that the fat man couldn't hit him without telegraphing his intention; Pearl did the same. Dumpy didn't do anything, his expression fearful. "You recognize me?" Ed asked.

"You look like every other bum down here." Ed's nostrils flared. His shoes and slacks together cost a little over $400. "If you're going to rob me, I only have about forty dollars in the back. You can have any clothes you want from the bins, and—"

Ed slapped Dumpy's Adam's apple, bulging the man's eyes as his hands flew up to his fat-ladened throat.

Ed gave him a moment, then, "Bet that felt like you swallowed a Toyota," he said matter-of-factly. "The next one will be harder and feel like you have a train caboose caught in your throat, and you might or might not survive it."

Pearl patted the man's fat, pimply arm and said motherly, "It will definitely feel like that, Dumpy. It's really, really icky."

"What are you talkin' about?" he managed, his voice strained, his mouth opening and closing to make the hurt in his throat stop. "Who the hell... What do you two want?" He lowered his chin to his chest as if expecting another blow.

"Let me introduce myself," Ed said, moving close to the man. He ducked his head and looked up into the man's red, tear-wet face. "My name is Ed. You sent me a package this evening."

The fat man's entire body jerked. He twisted halfway around as if to run to the lighted back room. But Ed stopped him by digging four stiffened and hooked fingers into the far side of Dumpy's Adam's apple. He yanked his hand back toward him. Ed knew the technique didn't tear loose the man's apple, but he knew from Dumpy's agonizing point of view he would be convinced it did.

Dumpy jackknifed forward, gagging on his own spit, snot, and panic. Pearl put the cherry on his anguish by slamming the sole of her shoe behind Dumpy's knee. The big man toppled heavily to the floor, writhing and gagging.

"Talk to him," Ed said. "I'm going to check his living quarters."

Pearl bent down and looked up into Dumpy's contorted red face. "Bet that feels like the whole train is in your throat now, huh?" The fat man's lips were wet and quivering, and unable to form a response.

The little room in the back was furnished with a broken-down vinyl sofa, a floor lamp, a box TV popular in the 1980s, and a leaning bookcase with sinking shelves stacked with pornographic magazines and, incongruously, large chunks of crystal quartz. A stove and a small refrigerator took up one corner of the room.

"Where is the woman? Where is Moxie?" Ed heard Pearl ask when Dumpy's gagging had slowed. No answer. Ed opened a closet door, revealing clothes collected from the bins out front, the stench of unwashed armpits clinging to the fabrics.

Ed assumed the room next to the refrigerator was the bathroom. The door was a poor fit, and he could see the light bleeding around its bottom and sides. He opened it.

"Mox," Ed breathed.

She was curled into a stained bathtub filled with about a foot of water, looking bizarre in her lovely robin-egg-colored winter coat that he liked and her black snow boots. Her face was smudged with red and smeared with eye makeup, no doubt from hours of crying and having her wrists tied painfully over her head to a rusty faucet, the fingers on her right hand wrapped with a blood-soaked rag. A dirty cloth that looked torn from the same material filled her mouth, bulging her cheeks. Faint animal sounds emitted from her throat as her body shook, rippling the water.

"I have her," He called to Pearl. "She's alive." He knelt on the floor by the tub and whispered, "You're okay now, Mox. I'm here." He gently removed the rag from her mouth and pulled the plug to release the water. She sobbed loudly as if the sound had been awaiting release.

"Oh, Ed," she said as if it hurt to speak. "That man…"

"We're going to get you out of here," he whispered as he untied her wrist restraints. Her left one flopped down next to her in the tub, but Ed caught her right wrist with the rag wrapped around her fingers and set it tenderly on her abdomen. "I've got you now, Mox; you're going to be fine."

Her eyes began to close, then opened wide. She looked at Ed as if seeing him for the first time. "I thought he was going...to kill...me. He kept saying he was going to kill—"

"Do you think you can stand?" She nodded. "Okay. I know your right hand is injured, so wrap your arm around my neck, and I'll help you stand. There's still some water on the bottom of the tub; we don't want you to slip."

"Do you want an ambulance?" Pearl called from the outer room.

"No. Make sure you have the key to the front door."

"I can see it in the lock."

It took several minutes for Ed to get Moxie to stand in the tub, step over the side with one foot and then the other. He let her rest in his arms for a minute before moving her a couple of steps toward the bathroom door, then stopped. "Pearl, I don't want her to see Dumpy." Ed realized he had just said Pearl's name aloud. But in this case, it didn't matter.

"Okay, gimme a sec." Ed heard a thump, like a fist hitting flesh. "Okay, we're good."

"Are you in a lot of pain?" Ed asked.

She nodded. "My hand, it burns like...fire. And he..." she shook her head, sobbing. "He touched me under my clothes."

Ed's mouth tightened as he held in his rage. "We'll be out of here in a sec, Mox. Then we'll get you—"

"He touched me, Ed. The bastard touched me repeatedly...all over."

Pearl called out, "All's good. When you come out, make a hard left and go around the other side of the center bins."

"Listen, Mox. We're going to walk out through the store. You won't have to see him. Okay?" She closed her eyes and nodded.

Her legs collapsed on their second step, but Ed quickly stopped her descent to the filthy floor. She wasn't big or overweight, but the sudden weight shift and his resistance hurt something in his back, making him sharply suck in his breath.

"Sorry, Ed. My legs are kind of—"

"Not a problem. Let's get you out of here." He saw Pearl's head partially above the top of a bin, indicating she was kneeling on the other side by Dumpy. Ed followed Pearl's directions, getting Moxie around the left side of the clothing container and almost to the door before her legs buckled for a second time. He gritted his teeth against what felt like a railroad spike penetrating his mid-vertebra.

"Sorry, Eddy," she whimpered, calling him that for the first time ever.

He strained to get them standing straight again. "I want you to get Mox to the truck, Pearl." By freely using her name, he told her that it didn't matter; she would know why. "I'll join you there in five minutes."

"I understand," she said. Ed could see her feet and Dumpy's extended legs by the bin. "Will you need me to help you? He's a fat pig."

"No." Two more steps and he and Moxie were at the front door. "Okay, Pearl, we're ready for you to take over." He looked at Moxie, her hooded eyes and slack mouth. He was glad that she was so out of it that she hadn't a clue what was happening. "Pearl is going to take you to her truck. I'll be there in a minute and sit with you."

Moxie's head rolled to the side and then straightened. "Pearl?" she managed upon seeing her. They liked each other.

"I got you, honey," Pearl said, picking up the blanket Ed had shrugged off when they first entered the store. She shook it, then wrapped it around Moxie's shoulders. "Let's get you to my truck. I got a fast heater."

"He cut off my finger."

"I'm so sorry," Pearl said as she supported Moxie out the doorway. "We'll get that fixed up. Don't you worry for a moment. We'll—"

Ed didn't hear the rest as he locked the door behind them and moved across the room to Dumpy, now sitting up against the bin, one hand gently caressing his throat.

"You have to stand for me, Dumpy. You're too big for me to muscle you up."

"O…okay," his voice was gravelly, his eyes unfocused. "Someone hit my throat, then that chick hit the side of my neck."

With Ed's help, the fat man eventually struggled to his feet. He swayed once as if to fall backward, but Ed stopped him. "Come on. Let's get you into your bathroom to splash some water on your face."

"Thank…you, that will…feel…" His coarse voice trailed off. Then, "That bitch was hot. But I think she hit my neck."

As they stagger-walked into the little apartment and headed toward the bathroom, Ed asked Dumpy why he cut off Moxie's finger. He seemed confused at first, but then his eyes refocused. "The woman said her friend Ed was rich and would pay to get her back. I thought sending this guy a finger would convince him I was serious."

They squeezed through the bathroom door and stopped by the sink. "I don't know who this Ed is. Do you?"

Ed nodded. "Yes, I do. It's me."

Dumpy frowned, his confusion coming and going. "Are you going to splash my face with water now?"

Ed shook his head, his cold eyes penetrating the fat man's.

Dumpy saw something in them that seemed to clear the fuzzies from his brain. "Wait, didn't you say you were this Ed a while ago?"

"I did."

"I don't understand. I thought I was going to get some water on my face—"

Ed eyed the tub's corner and quickly calculated the distance from it to Dumpy's temple. He knew from two hits in past years, the details of which he couldn't remember, that the pterion is the weakest part of the skull under which runs the meningeal artery. It was highly vulnerable to hard impact.

Dumpy turned his head and looked at Ed. "Why are we in here, mister? Wait, you're this Ed?"

"Turn back around, Dumpy." Ed looked at the tub's rounded porcelain again and the distance to the fat man's skull. "Step a little to the left. Okay, stop. Good. Perfect."

"Yes, I am 'this Ed.' And we're in here because this is where you will die. Do you understand what I'm saying, Dumpy? It's important you understand what will happen in a minute."

The fat man looked into Ed's eyes for a long moment. Then pathetically, "I guess I don't under—" He began to turn away, but Ed's firm grip on his fat upper arm stopped him. He looked at the hitman, his eyes comprehending.

"Ready, Dumpy?"

Chapter 9

Ed and Moxie rode together in the back seat of Pearl's big Dodge Ram pickup. He had wrapped his overcoat around the one she was wearing and scooted close so she could rest her head on his shoulder. It was a slow drive to the ER in the snow, which gave Ed time to speak slowly to Moxie so she could digest his words.

"This terrible situation is over, Mox. You're safe now and on the way to the hospital. That man will never hurt you again or anyone else. Do you understand?" He looked into the rearview mirror at Pearl's eyes looking back at them.

Moxie shook her head. "He was going to drown me in the tub because you didn't come. He said you didn't answer your phone."

"I didn't have it with me. I'm so sorry. But the man will never be in your life again. Do you understand?" She fell asleep without saying yes or no. He and Pearl didn't speak so as not to awaken her. When they got to the ER, Ed gently woke her and repeated his words. Her eyes looked a little clearer, but it was only for a moment because she began to tremble and frown as she looked around the truck, as if not understanding why she and Ed were in the backseat. Her wrapped hand twitched, and she sucked in her breath as a wave of pain passed through her.

"But I don't understand why we don't call the police, Ed. He hurt me and molested me, and he was going to—"

"You have to trust me, Mox. It's better this way, and you will never have to relive those awful hours to the police, the DA, your attorney, and the court. It's over now."

"I'm so dizzy; I think I need to throw up," she managed.

Ed barely got the door open in time.

The ER doctor bought Ed's story that Moxie had been preparing a meal and had severed her finger with a meat cleaver. Ed thought the explanation was weak, given the difficulty of hacking off a ring finger without nicking the little finger and middle finger. Still, the doctor, an old timer who had no doubt seen every possible way people hurt themselves, nodded. He asked where the finger was, and Ed said they didn't think to bring it in their panic. The doctor instructed him to get it and bring it to the ER ASAP.

Ed and Pearl drove to Spruce Grove, entered through the north side door, and went up to his apartment. He moved to the box on his kitchen counter, removed the lid, and pushed the tissue aside to reveal the finger with the attached ring

"Oh!" Pearl grunted, turning her head away. "That poor, poor lady. How godawful."

Ed pulled two tissues from a Kleenex box and wrapped the finger. He placed it into his overcoat pocket. "Let's get back to the ER."

At the hospital, the same nurse who had first met them looked at the finger and frowned. For a moment, Ed wondered if it might have been cut off hours earlier before he received it at Spruce Grove. If so, does the condition of the finger not coincide with his story? Before he could think of a cover story, the doctor came around the corner.

"That was quick," he said, smiling at Ed. "I thought the snow might have slowed you down." His glasses dangled from a cord around his neck. He lifted them to his eyes without putting them on and peered down at the finger in the bed of tissue the nurse held in her cupped hand. His eyes scanned the top of the finger and then used his pen to roll it over to examine the bottom. He looked up at Ed and Pearl.

Uh-oh, Ed thought.

"You two seem pretty cool about this."

Ed decided not to respond and hoped Pearl knew not to.

She did.

The doctor turned back to the finger, apparently accepting that he and Pearl were too tough cookies. "I'll give it a more thorough appraisal in surgery, but right now, I'm thinking all is good."

"Great news," Ed said, figuring he needed to say something. "God bless you, sir."

The doctor studied him for a few seconds longer than the situation required, Ed thought, then said in his smooth bedside manner, "She'll sleep until noon, so why don't you two go home and get some sleep? A nurse will call you."

As they pushed their way out the lobby doors, Pearl asked, "You think he was picking up a bad vibe from us?"

Ed shook his head. "He's been doing this for decades, so he probably has a highly tuned bullshit detector. And you did a good job not saying anything. Sometimes keeping quiet is the best response."

Pearl gave Ed a lift back to Spruce Grove. She asked him three times on the way if he was okay and if he would like her to stay with him. He assured her he was fine; he just needed to get some sleep. She reluctantly said okay, and they went their separate ways after a hug in the truck and a promise to meet up soon.

Ed had the best night's sleep he had had in a while. No dreams, no visitors on the balcony, and no memory flashes of Dumpy's head cracking on the tub.

He ate breakfast in his room to avoid seeing anyone. Angela called from the front office to check if he had heard from Moxie. Ed was glad it was her because she was the biggest gossip in the place, saving him from having to tell the story to everyone. He explained that she got home late and, while making a late salad in his room, had had a terrible accident with the cleaver. He took her to ER and was now waiting for a call from them.

After he hung up, he sipped his coffee and wondered if his ridiculous story would work. Moxie would want to tell everyone about the kidnapping and assault and, once she was clear-headed, argue with him about not reporting the incident to the police. She would also want to tell people that he and Pearl had rescued her. The obvious question listeners would have is what happened to the kidnapper. That would necessitate his lie getting longer and longer. That's when cracks would begin to appear. He couldn't let that happen.

The hospital called at 12:30 and said she was doing great and could go home at 1:30.

He walked two blocks to where he had left the tan Chevy four-door sedan before the snowfall. It belonged to a doctor friend and retired associate of The Organization. It had a false registration, altered VIN, and plates. Ed borrowed it from time to time, often keeping it for extended periods if no one else needed it.

At the hospital, a nurse told Ed that Moxie's heartbeat had accelerated rapidly for 30 minutes around 5 a.m. but returned to normal just as quickly. "Doctor James says it was probably tachycardia, a common stress response. She's fine now, but her blood pressure is higher than we like."

"There's a retired nurse at Spruce Grove who checks people's blood pressure regularly. I'll ask her to monitor it."

The nurse nodded. "That's perfect. Oh, by the way, Moxie thinks she was kidnapped by a fat man who cut her finger off and was going to drown her in a rusty bathtub."

Ed nodded grimly. "Did she also mention that she is a famous actress in Hollywood and won an Academy Award for a movie she made with Alfred Hitchcock?" He shook his head to emphasize his sadness about her issue. "Sometimes her imagination gets away from her."

The nurse nodded. "Some patients swear they were abducted by aliens and want us to look for embedded microchips." When Ed concluded his polite chuckle, the nurse said, patting his arm, "Well, she is blessed she has you in her life."

Ed shook his head. "No, no. It's me who is blessed."

She said the doctor reattached the finger, but it wasn't a 100 percent guaranteed save and would necessitate multiple follow-up appointments and possibly another surgery.

Moxie was sitting on the edge of the bed when Ed entered her room, her finger splinted and wrapped so thickly it nearly doubled the size of her hand. She didn't smile at him and didn't acknowledge that he was standing in the room as a young nurse situated her in a wheelchair. As the nurse double-checked that she had everything out of the closet, Moxie finally looked at Ed, her look blank as if he were a stranger. The nurse told Ed to bring his car around to the lobby doors.

This wasn't good, Ed thought, getting behind the wheel. He didn't know what to do, but he certainly couldn't let a crazy thing like this be his downfall. He did have one thought, a dark one, and he hated himself for thinking it.

At the hospital entrance, he and the nurse situated Moxie in the front seat. Ed thanked her, and they were on their way. After several blocks, Moxie still hadn't said a word. Ed broke the silence. "That man is gone now, Mox. Some buddies of mine took him to the train station."

In his peripheral, Ed could see her study him for a long moment before turning back to look out her side window. She's not buying it, he thought.

"Okay," she said finally, her head still turned away from him. She crossed her arms, cupped her elbows in her palms, and leaned away until she was against the passenger door.

He wanted to ask her how she got to Dumpy's store but thought it best not to bring it up. His store was only a few blocks north of Ellen's, a rapidly deteriorating area that stood in stark contrast to the high-end store where she had been shopping. Dumpy probably spotted Moxie in the store or coming out of it and assumed she had money based on her expensive-looking clothes. Ed had seen her quiver and shake on more than one occasion when a street person asked them for a handout. She must have been too frightened or shocked to shout or scream when Dumpy demanded she come with him.

Florence would have kicked his nuts into his chest cavity.

How much of that does Moxie remember? Judging by the look she gave him when he explained about Dumpy being escorted to a train and that he would never return, coupled with her simple "okay," she wasn't buying his explanation one bit. Who would? It was ridiculous.

Add to the goat rope was that he had already told nurses, the doctor, and people at Spruce Grove that she had cut her finger while cooking.

He had never screwed up a situation as much as he had this one.

At Spruce Grove, he walked Moxie to her room, happily not running into other tenants, and helped her settle in. He tried to get her to lie down, but she complained she was slept out and just wanted to sit in her favorite chair that looked out onto her balcony. She asked him to sit in his usual place beside her.

After a few minutes of silence, Moxie spoke. "Okay, here it is," she said with a sigh. She looked at him, and he at her. "I need a break in our relationship."

Ed looked at her, his face expressionless, though he could feel butterflies flitting about in his chest, free and happy.

"Things don't feel right to me, Ed, and that's on top of what I shared with you yesterday. Or was it two days ago?" She closed her eyes and shook her head. "God, I've lost all sense of time after everything that's happened. Anyway, I'm talking about when I told you about me feeling like I don't know anything about you, your past." She paused, looking out of her partially iced-over glass door at her snow-covered balcony, but he could tell she was looking at him out of the corner of her eyes. If she expected him to say something in his defense, he wouldn't.

"We can't help seeing each other around the home, so we'll just nod or wave from across the room. I need this, Ed; I think we need this."

He didn't say anything for what he thought was an appropriate amount of time, then, "Okay, Mox. Let's do that. But if you need anything, promise you'll let me know. I'm just two doors down."

She nodded, her eyes tearing, then turned to look out the glass door. She lifted her good hand from her lap, patted her chest, then lightly massaged her upper left arm.

Ed got up, touched her shoulder, and headed toward the door, his eyes smiling.

Chapter 10

Ed was sitting at his little kitchen table enjoying tea. One of the ladies—Dixie, a painfully skinny little thing with a broken nose earned when she boxed for a couple years in the Army during WWII—gave him a package of pine needle tea a few weeks ago. He thanked her kindly, saying that he had never heard of it. She said she had just recently tried it and liked it.

"It's good for the digestion, Ed," she said. "At first, I was concerned they hadn't cleaned the bird shit off the needles, but if they didn't, it's still good, anyhow. Just extra chewy."

There was no mention of Dumpy's death in the news. An accidental fall isn't news in a crime-ridden city like Portland, Oregon. Even if there had been suspicion, Ed had confidence in his "scene cleaning." After 70-some jobs, he knew how to remove any trace of his presence with perfection and speed.

He hadn't had time to think about Dumpy in the last day and a half, at least not much. He hadn't talked with Pearl about it, as he hadn't seen or heard from her since she brought him back to Spruce Grove. He had taught her that it was a wise routine for partners to avoid each other for a while after a job. Attention to the smallest precautions had kept him out of prison for three decades.

When the image of Dumpy's head smashing against the edge of the old bathtub did pass through his mind—twice, to be exact—his only thought was how easy his decision was to kill him. It wasn't how he did it; he had always been creative, never once duplicating his modus operandi. It was the speed of his decision to do it that was giving him pause. It was quick and without internal argument.

Why was he thinking about that now at this late date? He had long ago found a place in his mind that allowed him to do the job without conscience.

One of his motivations to terminate was that if he let the man live and called the police from Dumpy's place, his name and Pearl's would be in the police reports. Kidnapping a well-to-do female senior citizen for ransom, chopping off her finger, sexually molesting her, and attempting to drown her would be big news, not only in Portland but probably nationwide. He and Pearl would be hailed heroes, and their photos would be all over. Cops and reporters would likely investigate their backgrounds, finding nothing. The Organization did a fine job removing their agents' footprints—false identity, fingerprints, and DNA—from everywhere. He knew Cull did the same for its agents. So any attempt to dig up info on them would end with a big fat zero.

Of course, a suspicious detective or news reporter would see a big fat zero as a red flag. It might be understandable for either Pearl or him to come up clean, but would it be for two people who happened to be together? No, the press would see this as a second story. And there was a good chance that someone between New England and Southern California would alert on his photo and remember where he saw him. "Hey, I remember that guy. He was dressed to the nines and had hard eyes like those in the picture. But where did I see him? Oh yeah, it was near where that poor sap was stabbed with hedge shears."

No, it was cleaner to snuff Dumpy and rid the world of a terrible person at the same time.

Then there was the story he told Mox about his buddies shipping Dumpy off on a train. While he knew many people, he didn't have any buddies, and she knew that. She had been dopey from her medications when he told her. Ed's thinking, based on a hunch more than science, was that if he convinced her when she was high, she would come out of the drug haze still believing him.

Yes, it was a weak plan, so it might be time for him to move out of Portland, establish a new ID, and find a nice retirement home in Maui. Florence loved Hawaii.

Ed spent the rest of the day sitting in his chair in front of the glass balcony door, dozing, and reading a James Lee Burke novel. Florence introduced him to Burke's work, and he had read about a dozen of his tales from the South. The man captured the human condition flawlessly. He wondered how Burke would describe him. Aloud, Ed mused, "The hitman was as worn down as an old boot, the scuff marks and cracks in his face revealing a lifetime of good and evil and life and death. But through it all, he tried his best to be on the side of good." He smiled to himself, and said aloud, "That's pretty good, and it's true."

An image of Dumpy's distorted face impacting the bathtub's corner flashed in front of him and remained. The man was immensely repellant:

He was morbidly obese, his torso a 50-gallon barrel of fat, and his large cranium carried so much blubber that it turned his eyes into slits and rolls of it piled under his jaw and at the back of his neck. Even his feet were fat.

Why was he thinking about Dumpy this time?

Did focusing on the man's unpleasant appearance help justify killing him—which he did as easily as twisting his foot on a nasty cockroach? Or as easily as Chick Norris, the black rooster, did with the rat? Was Chick really defending the chickens from the rat? The rodent was only eating pieces of grain when Ed looked down from the hall window. He wasn't a threat to the chickens. But the rooster attacked anyway, without pondering his actions at all. He stabbed it mercilessly with his dagger of a spur, then parked himself a few feet away, looking about the pen, before slowly turning his gaze up at him.

So swift the rooster had killed, so violently, so easily.

The same way he had killed Dumpy.

Ed inhaled deeply, mentally drawing Dumpy and all his thoughts and images surrounding the man into his lungs, then forcefully exhaled them into the room. A shrink on a daytime talk show suggested doing that to eliminate negativity. There might be something to it. He felt better. Not much, just a little.

He had been examining his human condition of late. Ed accepted that there were fewer miles ahead than he had already traveled. At times, he was bothered thinking no one would remember him except a few oldsters here at Spruce Grove. He had no family, no close friends, just the folks here—and soon they would be gone too. When the last one who knew him passed, so would be the end of his existence.

And that was okay because his life's work hadn't been about celebrity. His destiny was to rid the world of over six dozen terrible human beings. If he hadn't done his work, each of those still living would have interacted destructively with others, and the effects would have spread exponentially.

He had to take comfort in that legacy, one known only to him. Most of the time, he did, but of late, it's been taking bites out of his soul. Might that explain the hallucinations?

He ate dinner in his room, watched the news, and went to bed early.

At 3 a.m., the hallucinations returned.

Chapter 11

Ed was sleeping on his back, facing the ceiling, when a sound jolted him awake. "What…?" he mumbled into the darkness. The sound was… He frowned; he didn't know what it was. It continued as his brain cleared a little, but not enough to know if he was awake or dreaming. He just wanted to sleep.

The repetitive sound grew louder.

In his sleep-clouded brain, it was like someone was slapping something, making whatever it was rattle after each impact. Glass, maybe? Yeah, like someone was hitting his window. He forced his eyes to open wider as he struggled for clarity. But he didn't have a window—only the sliding glass door.

The slapping was louder now, more desperate.

Fully awake, Ed came up on his elbow and looked toward the door.

Dumpy.

The fat man was standing on the balcony outside the door, his palm smacking the glass rhythmically, the side of his head pressed against the door as if to show Ed the fruits of his work: his concave skull near his ear, blood streaming down over his jawline and dripping onto his T-shirt. He turned toward Ed, his huge belly pushing against the glass, his palm continuing to slap the door over and over and over.

"You're not real," Ed said, pushing the covers away. He turned on the lamp. It reflected in the glass door; next to it, Dumpy, his mouth moving without audio. Ed moved quickly toward it, more angry than afraid. He pushed the sliding door open, banging it against its stop.

The fat man was gone.

The snow-covered balcony floor was undisturbed, and a thin layer on the door was also untouched.

He took a deep breath and let it out, his breath fog blowing back into his face. He went inside, slipped on his slippers, and retrieved a broom. He carried it back to the still-open glass door and began sweeping a pathway to the balcony guard rail. The cold wasted little time penetrating Ed's body, instantly aching his joints and fingers.

Down below, the walkway lights and the accent glow from the balconies cast a ghostly gloom on the snow-covered yard and spruce trees, their limbs sagging helplessly from the weight. A dozen trees dotted the yard. The falling snow, whipped about by the wind, made it impossible to see with clarity the farthest ones. But the five closest trees Ed could see easily—as well as the figures standing by each trunk, their dead faces looking up at him.

He had seen this surreal sight before, but still, he sucked in the frozen air and dropped the broom silently on the snow-covered floor. He stepped back quickly, one step, two, three...

He backed over the threshold into his room and forcefully slid the glass door closed, the thud jarring, the impact knocking askew an 8 x 10 framed painting of a raven on the wall next to the door.

Ed knew the apparitions would be unseen by anyone looking down from their balconies because they belonged solely to him, his mind, and his eyes; he was responsible for them. And he knew they would be there if he again peered down on the grounds.

The room had chilled the few minutes the door was open, making visible his breath. He climbed back into his bed but sat up, his back against the wall and the covers pulled up to his chest. Incongruously, or maybe not, he remembered a biography he read years ago titled, *The Hammer* by an assassin using a penname of Jonathan K. Hammer. Three things stuck in Ed's mind about the book: Hammer had completed only half as many hits as he had, and while the man felt his missions served a greater good, they tormented him to the brink of insanity.

The final sentence in the last chapter read, "They come back."

Ed wasn't about to go back out onto the balcony. He needed to get control of his mind. He had done a little meditating of late, finding it relaxing but mostly enjoying the feeling of being in the moment. The meditation guides always say to be, "Right here, right now," When you're right here, right now, the past is in the past, and the future hasn't happened yet. He needed to get a better handle on that. Because—

Out the glass door, across the balcony, and over the rail, the snow-covered tree tops visible from his bed lit up with strobing red lights. He had never seen them this late before because he was always asleep, but he had many other times, at least twice a week in the evening. The red whipping lights belonged to ambulances responding to an emergency call at Spruce Grove.

Some day they will come for him, Ed thought before turning off his nightstand light and shutting his eyes, hoping for dreamless sleep.

Ed had awakened at 6 a.m., though the fitful three hours after his rude awakening could hardly be called "sleep." It was 7:10 now, and he was sitting in his recliner working on his fourth cup of coffee and looking out at the balcony, his broom-swept pathway to the railing and the treetops beyond it. The snow had stopped, and the sky showed patches of blue, but the dark clouds looked heavy and would no doubt soon dominate.

The events of last night seemed far away and unreal. But they were real, at least in his psyche. The hallucinations were happening too often of late, and that worried him. And it scared him, as much as he hated admitting it. But he refused to lose himself to his fear. He never had in his life, and he wouldn't now.

The four cups of caffeine had given him the jitters but didn't do much for his sleep deprivation. Ed slapped his cheeks, stretched his eyes wide, and moved his head from side to side, cracking his spine. That didn't help, either.

He thought about Mox. What if she didn't buy his explanation about running Dumpy out of town? What if she had a gut feeling about how he dealt with the man? Didn't she say something about her feeling an aura of danger emanating from him yesterday morning in the rec room?

What a can of worms. What an irony after never coming close to getting caught on all his jobs, only to crash and burn on this unplanned goat rope.

He wouldn't get caught if no one believed her.

He wouldn't get caught if Mox kept quiet.

He wouldn't get caught if she never got the chance to tell her story... Or if she couldn't tell it.

On that thought, he dozed off and dreamt of the black rooster killing the rat with its spur.

Chapter 12

Ed was down the hall from his room, waiting for the elevator. When the doors finally slid open, he was debating looking out the window to check on the chickens—and the rooster.

"Hold the door, Ed."

He thought it was Mox for a second, though it wasn't her voice; it belonged to Lori Sue, who lived in the apartment all the way down the hall. He had tea with her a few months ago and learned she had been a singer with the Tunetts, an African American trio in the late 1950s. The group broke up just before Motown exploded on the music scene.

She smiled at Ed, then frowned with a look of concern. "Poor Moxie, Ed. My goodness, how horrible. I heard someone say that—oh yes, it was Carmella—that she was abducted by some brute and her finger severed—"

"That didn't happen, Lori Sue. It was a cooking accident with a cleaver. She's heavily medicated, you see. Please tell the others that, would you?"

"Oh my. The poor dear. Yes, yes, of course, I'll spread the word. Carmilla said she spoke with Moxie on the phone last night, and Moxie told her she was going to stay in her room for a day or two."

"Good," he said aloud, immediately wishing he hadn't said it with an exhalation of relief.

Lori Sue touched Ed's arm. "I know what that's like to be so drugged out of your mind." She leaned in and whispered conspiratorially. "Just between you and me and some good weed, I love that feeling. If you ever want to get together and do some edibles."

"Sounds tempting, Lori Sue. But right now, I got to get downstairs. Have a lovely day."

She wiggled her fingers goodbye as the door swooshed shut, apparently forgetting she was going to ride down.

"Shitshitshitshit," he said aloud. "Moxie's mouth is going to bring everything crashing down. I need to stop her—this morning."

"Oh, Ed!" The front desk person, Connie, called out as he stepped out of the elevator. She had been standing in her office doorway. She hurried over to him, her eyes tearing. "I'm so sorry about your Moxie," she embraced him, taking him by surprise and not knowing what to do with his arms.

Dani, 85 years old and POW-skinny, stopped her wheelchair next to him and took his hand. "My thought and prayers are with you, Ed."

"Thank you," he said. "But listen, Moxie's a little confused—"

Ben, the old bastard on the balcony Ed had exchanged words with when he woke up in the snow, swerved his wheelchair over and clanked his against Dani's.

"Hey," Dani said irritably. "You're so rude, Ben."

"You'll get over it," he said dismissively. He looked up at Ed. "Shit happens, old boy. Come by my room later, and I'll buy you a beer." He banged Dani's chair again, then continued toward the elevator without commenting.

Ed looked at Dani and Connie. "Thank you for your kind words, ladies, but she wasn't kidnapped. We were cooking in my room and—"

Connie placed her palm on Ed's chest. "Ed." He looked at her, surprised by the gesture. "My goodness," she said. "You don't know."

"Oh, my," Dani breathed.

Ed frowned. "What?"

"I'm so sorry, Ed," Connie said. "Moxie passed last night. I'm so sorry to be the one to have to tell you."

The flashing red lights bouncing off the treetops in the middle of the night, Ed thought.

Connie went on. "Libby, her neighbor, heard a crash coming from Moxie's room about two forty-five or so. Libby called her, but when she didn't get an answer, she went over and knocked on her door. Again, no answer. So Libby called Sylvia down here at the front desk. Sylvia took Charlie up to her room because he has passkeys. Anyway, they found her lying across her nightstand. It's where she fell, see? And it knocked everything off. That was the crash, you see."

"I'm thinking her poor old heart gave out," Dani said. "When I talked to her briefly yesterday, she complained about her left arm hurting, and she kept patting her chest, just as Ronald, my late husband, did, may he rot in hell. Anyway, poor Moxie. It was the shock of losing a finger, I bet. That's rough."

Ed didn't know what expression he was wearing, but he felt a strange cocktail blend of sadness, shock, and giddy relief.

"Someone said that you two were talking about marriage," Dani said, rubbing the back of his hand. "So sorry, Ed. It's just so awful."

He needed to get away from these two. "Thanks, ladies," he whispered. "I'm heading back up. And if you'd be so kind, please tell people I need some alone time." He took a couple of steps, then turned back to Connie. "Is she in her apart— Have they removed…"

Connie nodded. "They did, Ed," she said gently. "Around four this morning. Again, I'm so sorry. And My God, why didn't someone come and notify you then? I'll rip into the night staff, I promise."

He nodded and headed toward the elevator, deliberately slumping his shoulder to look sad.

He made a cup of white tea, and for once, not one lady had dropped off pastry in the last couple of days. He would probably get a butt load now, a high-calorie sympathy gift, and the hope that the giver's name remains in his mind as an available replacement. He carried his cup to his recliner, sat back, and levered the footrest.

Mox. He wasn't sure what to think right now. He wasn't feeling any emotion at all about her death. It may be too early. After all, he just learned of it a few minutes ago. Or, had his ability to control his emotions, polished over the years as a survival tool, dulled his feelings even about someone he cared for? They weren't dulled when it came to Florence. He still grieved her passing. Apparently, his cloaked sentiments hand-picked situations for him to feel and not feel.

Over the years, he had learned to control his mind after a job, an ability that had kept him relatively sane. Lately, for some unknown reason, the protective shield he had built had weakened, collapsed even. To his chagrin, memories of all those hits had returned like scenes from a B-grade horror movie. And, to karma's amusement, they waited to appear until he was almost an octogenarian, and the Grim Reaper was rubbing his cold palms together in eager anticipation of taking him to a party. It would be a gala event where he would be the guest of honor, and the party-goers would be those folks he hurried to an early death.

Ed sipped his tea, looking contemplatively out the glass door. After a moment, he came back to the present and chuckled at himself. I'm an old man remembering, like a geezer sitting on a weathered bench on the sun-side of a country store, sharing swigs from a bottle of inexpensive whiskey with another oldster and swapping lies about their days in the spotlight.

Ed had never had a buddy. He couldn't. What could he share with him? It would be a friendship based on lies, a made-up life, in which he would have to stay true to the untruth. Did he miss having a pal? It was a thought he had never considered, or if he had, he had quickly brushed it aside as something to think about later. The answer... Yeah, he missed having one.

Snow began falling again, He had never tried to act younger than his age. He often mimicked being lame or, in some way, feeble as part of a disguise. But now he suddenly felt old, lonely, and the weight of his years. At least Mox had kept the loneliness away. A little.

He pushed down the leg rest, began to get up but changed his mind, and flopped back, adjusting himself for comfort. So tired, he thought. So very...

A car horn sounded; Model A Ford, 1927 vintage, jerked Ed awake into darkness. Where am I? Outside the glass sliding door, the balcony light illuminated the falling snow accumulating on the floor and railing. "My apartment," he said aloud. He twisted around and looked at the microwave clock. 5:15 p.m.

He had slept all day. The old car horn sounded again, shrill, nerve jarring, anxious. He got up quickly, switched on the nightstand lamp, and snatched his phone off the bed.

It was Pearl. He had called the burner phone number after receiving Mox's finger in a box. "Is everything okay?"

"Are you alone?" Her voice was tight and breathy, an octave higher than her norm.

"Yes."

Silence. Then, "I'm working."

Was that fear he was hearing in her voice?

"Oh, God... I've..."

Yes, fear and distress.

"I could use some assistance."

Cryptic, and the same words he had used when he called her to help find Moxie.

"Location?" he asked, heading to his closet. He pulled out a pair of black, Cali leather boots, $220.00, and Softshell pants, black, $115.00.

"Freeway, heading northbound toward your city."

His pants and boots on, he slipped into his ash-colored Canada Goose Expedition Parka. She said she was working. "Is the principal visible?"

"A quarter mile in the lead. The traffic is virtually non-existent in this weather. Can you..." She inhaled sharply. Then, "Can you help me"

He spotted Mox's Arctic Down gloves he had given her last Christmas on the closet's top shelf. His black Marco lambskin gloves had proved worthless a few days ago when he was standing across the street from Annie's café as the snow began to fall. The Arctic Downs were women's gloves, but much warmer than his. Plus, they had the touch screen feature that let him use his phone without taking them off.

"I have the sedan. Where exactly are you?" He pushed aside his hanging clothes to reveal a four-foot-long chest. He had been keeping it in his storage area in the basement, but after a couple of tenants had things stolen, he moved it to his closet until he could figure out where to keep it.

Again, a deep, ragged breath intake. Then, "A little north of Salem."

"Give me a minute, okay?" He tapped in the code on the lock, an audible click followed, and the latch released. The interior of the box contained two shelves. The top one held 12 knives, all serving a different purpose, all evenly spaced on a felt, burgundy liner. The least expensive blade cost him $9.99; the priciest $499.99. What he wanted was on the second shelf.

Ed removed the top shelf and set it on the floor. The second one displayed two hatchets, one medieval looking; he didn't know or care if they were authentic. The other was genuine, a chopper from a Mohican tribe that lived around Pittsfield, Massachusetts, in the early 1700s. The third weapon was a Cold Steel War Hammer. It wasn't an antique, but a similar version used in days of old against an adversary wearing armor.

He wrapped his hand around the handle and picked it up, abruptly stopping in mid-lift. He pondered why he was retrieving it. It wasn't because the hammer part consisted of four striking heads. No, that wasn't it. He took a ragged breath, remembering that he had thought about the curved steel spike on the back of the weapon when he watched the rooster kill the rat. The hammer's metal spur was nearly identical to Chick Norris's long killing spur behind his claws.

An image of the rooster, its spur dripping red, looking up at him flashed across his mind, the fowl's eyes soulless, communicating, *see what I did there, hitman?*

Ed shook his head to clear the thought away.

He snapped the leather cover securely over the spur end and dropped it into his deep overcoat pocket. The handle had been 30 inches long, but he had cut it down, so the entire weapon was a more manageable 15 inches. The black handle still extended above his pocket a few inches, but his coat was black too, so it was less obvious.

"You there?" he asked, pushing open his apartment door. He headed for the stairs to avoid running into anyone and to stay out of sight of the front desk person checking to see who was coming out of the elevator so late.

He heard only heavy breathing.

"You there?" he repeated.

"Yes. Still…on the…freeway. Wilsonville is coming up in about 15 minutes or less. I…don't know where…he's going."

Ed had slipped out the side door unseen and trudged toward the parking lot. "Are you okay? You don't sound okay."

Silence.

Then a deep, ragged breath before whispering, "He…shot me."

Chapter 13

"What? He shot—"

"I'm doing okay. The bullet…hit the top of my shoulder. Grooved… It grooved a path then went out the back side." Sound of a deep inhalation. "I can function, but it burns like hell. It's kinda hard…to lift it, my arm, I mean. Maybe it tore through nerves and tendons, or something."

It took Ed three attempts to pin his phone between his ear and shoulder. He fumbled through his coat pockets for the car's electronic key fob. "Found it." He didn't mean to say that aloud. He was breathing hard. The words 'He shot me' jumbled his thinking and physical coordination.

"Huh? Found wha—"

The phone slipped off his shoulder and dropped into the snow before he could catch it. "Damn!" The car's shadow blocked the walkway light, preventing him from seeing where precisely it fell. He pointed the key fob at the car door.

Nothing happened. Had the release function in the door frozen up?

"Hold on," he shouted, hopefully, loud enough that Pearl heard.

"Come on," he said aloud, pressing the fob each time he jabbed it at the door and not getting a response. He tried again, and the lock released, the sound as sluggish and cold as he felt. He muscled the door open with a crackling sound of breaking ice, then commenced feeling around in the snow for his phone. Bending down, he could hear Pearl's faraway voice, her words muffled, as he felt about in the 10-inch-deep drift.

"Hold on. I'm looking for the…got it!" It had sunk only partway into the snow and was undamaged. "Talk to me," he said into it, climbing into the 12-year-old Chevy and inserting the key. The key, he thought, shaking his head at his frustration, an emotion he rarely felt. I could have opened the door with it.

"Did you hear any of what I said?"

The car started with a slow groan. He switched on the wipers, but they wouldn't move.

"One more second."

Ed set the phone on the passenger seat and got back out. "Fuck!" he heard Pearl say, her voice perturbed and far away.

He brushed the snow off the windshield, climbed back in, turned up the heater full blast, and picked up the phone. He heard only heavy breathing. "I'm back. Be cryptic."

Silence, then, "I thought… You didn't say anything." There was an edge of panic in her voice.

"Sorry, I had a bit of an issue."

"I'm… I'm still on him. A sign a ways back said, 'Wilsonville, five miles.'"

"Okay, I'm on the road. I'll catch the freeway on Thirty-Ninth street. How bad is your pain?"

"I can function. The pain has subsided now, but my arm is hanging dead. He came at me—"

"Tell me how it happened later. Right now, we need a plan to get him."

"Damn, it's hurting again and—"

"Eat the pain; you hear me? Pain wants to distract you from your mission. Think of a big circle. Now put a dot in the circle near the bottom. You see it?"

Deep, ragged breath. "Kinda."

"That dot is your pain. Understand?"

"Mine is bigger than that—"

"Think: That dot is my pain, that dot is my pain, that dot is my pain. Over and over, until you believe it. The rest of the space in the circle is your mission. Now *our* mission. You copy?"

"Okay."

"Good. Where are you now?"

"Two miles to Wilsonville. But…"

"But?"

"There's been this van messing with me. Two guys, twenties. They matched…my speed about twenty miles back, throwing kisses and gesturing…for me to pull over. They did that for about a half mile, then backed off to about an eighth mile or so behind me. It's light tan with one headlight that's real dim."

"Okay."

"It's been behind me for about fifteen minutes." Her breathing was still ragged, but she was better focused.

"Okay. There are always flies in the ointment. It just means your mission has been modified to watching the pickup in front of you and the van behind you. No heavy lifting, just watch."

"Where are you?" she asked, her voice now calm but with a tinge of worry.

"I'm on the freeway too but going south. I'm to your front, so that's good. In four miles, I'm going to take the Salmon Bridge exit, and, hopefully, the traffic is light on it, so I can park on top and watch for you coming my way."

"Okay. I think that exit is about five miles from where I am now. The Benz is going about 20 miles per hour. He must be a nervous driver in the snow."

"A Mercedes-Benz?"

"Yeah, black."

"Okay. The snow's coming down harder, and the visibility is getting worse. Do this for me. A half mile from the exit, activate your left turn signal. I'll let you know when I'm close."

"I'll have to use my left hand because my right—"

"The mission. We focus on the mission."

Ed could barely make out a solo vehicle in front of him, a large semi. In his rearview mirror, he could count three sets of dim headlights far behind him.

After about five minutes of silence, Ed said, "Okay, there's the sign for my exit, a quarter mile."

"I'm half a mile or so. He's still creeping along."

Ed glided onto the ramp, slipped to a stop at the top, and turned left with a slight fishtail onto the overpass. There were no other cars in either direction on it. He stopped midway across the overpass, got out, and walked to the guardrail. "I'm in place on the overpass. Hit your turn signal anytime when you see your exit."

Visibility was about an eighth of a mile, less when a wind gust blew the snow falling sideways across the lanes. There wasn't traffic going southbound, but Ed could make out a set of headlights heading toward him. Closer, closer...there it was. The Mercedes, and a ways behind it, Pearl's white truck and her flashing left turn signal.

"I see you and the Mercedes—"

"He's taking the Salmon Bridge exit," Pearl said loudly into his ear.

"What are the odds?" Ed said, keeping his voice calm, hoping to keep Pearl mellow. He moved around the front of his car and climbed in.

"What...do we...do?" Pearl said, each word loud and breathy.

She's getting rattled again, Ed thought. "You already know. We do the mission and deal with whatever comes up. Turn off your turn signal," he said calmly. "Slow down, then take the exit after he reaches the top of the ramp. It's curved, so he can't see you from the top. I'll take over the lead follow, and you stay far behind me. This will give him a different visual in his mirror. All will be good."

"He can probably go left or right at the top." She sounded calmer.

"If he goes right, I'll proceed in the direction my car is already pointing, and follow from a ways back. You follow me. If he goes left, across the overpass, I'll go forward until he can't see me in his mirror, then I'll crank a U-turn. You wait for a beat before you follow me from a ways back."

"I'm stopped at the bottom now, and I can't see him. Shit, the van turned too, and it's stopping right behind me."

"Let's focus on the principal and keep the van in your peripheral. If you can't see the principle, he can't see you. Wait until I tell you what's happening. Okay, I can see a pair of headlights shining across the bridge to my front. He's not moving, probably deciding which way to go. That probably means taking the ramp was a last-minute decision."

"I don't know if these assholes behind me will get out."

"Okay, the principal is making a left, coming my way. Wait until I proceed forward and get far enough that he can't see me in his mirror. Then I'll crank a U-turn. When I pass you, you follow a ways behind me. The leapfrog technique gives him a different vehicle in his rearview mirror. I'll hang back far enough that he only sees my headlights."

"Ed?" She gasped. "Oh shit. Sorry."

No need to admonish her, Ed thought. She knows she said my name. He used his periphery to look at the driver as they passed each other, but the Mercedes's windows were too tinted to see any detail other than a figure behind the wheel.

Ed squinted from the glare of Pearl's pickup lights as he passed the top of the offramp. He looked at his rearview mirror to see how far the Mercedes had gone. "No!" he said loudly into the phone as she guided her pickup off the ramp and onto the bridge, heading the same way the Mercedes was going.

Ed exhaled his frustration. She was supposed to wait for him to turn around and return to take the lead. And now the tan van was making a left turn onto the overpass, too, between Pearl and him. He couldn't see the van's interior that well, but his impression was two men were in it. Were they associates of the principal?

"Sorry, Ed," Pearl said, again using his name. "I got rattled and didn't wait for you to pass. I… don't have an excuse."

"We'll make it work," he said calmly, doing a good job of hiding his frustration.

With the pickup and van between the Mercedes and him, Ed decided the principal's line of sight was blocked enough for him to make a U-turn now. Snow had stuck to his driver's side window, so he zipped it down to see his outside mirror as he began his turn.

He heard a revving engine and sliding tires. It came from the overpass ahead of him.

Ed stopped halfway into his turn, his backend facing south, his front north, which allowed him to look down the overpass to where the Mercedes was spinning its tires backward up the southbound, wrong-way ramp. He wasn't the only one confused.

Pearl stopped about 10 yards back from the ramp, her snow tires having better traction than the principal's $80,000 vehicle. The van had zero traction and slid sideways toward the Dodge Ram's rear. It stopped short of crunching its rear driver's side into the pickup tailgate.

Thinking his sideways position made him a large target, Ed swung his car around until its front end faced the others. He crept forward, stopping half a dozen yards short of the van, so he could watch and react should things go down the toilet, which his gut told him was imminent.

As the Mercedes' tires continued to spin, the vehicle following Pearl shuddered a little. Ed couldn't see the driver's side of the van since it was sideways to him, but he guessed the driver had exited.

The Mercedes' tires caught hold, lurching the car backward up the ramp, then into a reverse turn onto the overpass. It accelerated faster and faster until it smashed into the Dodge Ram's front end.

There was a heartbeat of heavy silence, then a low-volume *fump fump fump fump.*

Holes appeared in the Mercedes-Benz's back window. Ed remembered Pearl telling him she had a sound suppressor for her Glock.

As he goosed his car forward to help Pearl, several things happened in rapid succession.

The van's passenger exited, male, early 20s, wearing a red sweatshirt and a backward baseball cap. He moved toward the front of the van and disappeared around its front.

The Mercedes driver bailed out a second later, mid-40s and wearing a dark blue P-coat. He pointed a semi-auto at Pearl's windshield.

A young man wearing an orange ski jacket stepped away from the driver's side of the van. Didn't he hear the muffled gunshots?

The Mercedes driver fired twice at Pearl's windshield, took two quick steps to the side of the truck, and fired two more rounds at the driver's side window.

Ed leaned toward his passenger seat, his head just high enough to see over his dash with one eye. He thought he heard Pearl cry out, but he couldn't be sure.

The gunman swung his barrel toward the van's driver, now backing up quickly and screaming, "Wait wait wait!" his arms extended toward the man as if that would ward off a bullet.

It didn't.

The impact snapped the young man's head so far back that Ed could see the hole in his forehead as he crumpled onto the snowy overpass.

The gunman sidestepped enough to see the front end of the van. He double-tapped two rounds. Ed couldn't see that side of the vehicle, but he heard a grunt followed by a piercing scream.

Ed sat up, reaching for the shift to slam it into Drive and launch the Chevy into the shooter just as the man looked his way. Ed threw himself back across the passenger seat a hair of a second before a round punched through the top center of his windshield, blowing apart the rearview mirror and spraying plastic and glass over Ed.

Fump! Another muffled shot sounded like Pearl's weapon, followed by a loud groan and a curse. The voice was male, hopefully the Mercedes driver.

Silence. Then a volley of thump *fump fump fump*, as Pearl's weapon sent more rounds.

The sound of a revving engine and of a vehicle spinning its tires, the sound fading.

Ed tentatively looked over the dash just in time to see the Mercedes's taillights, small in the distance beyond the overpass, disappear around a curve to the left. "Pearl," Ed whispered, his heart thumping.

He pushed open his car door just as Pearl opened hers and climbed down. They looked at each other. Her left jacket sleeve was wet with blood, and her right sleeve was saturated with it. Pearl's arm hung along her side as she pointed her weapon with her left at the van driver crumpled on the ground.

"I got him," Ed said since he was standing closest. "Check the passenger." He slipped off Moxie's right glove and pressed two fingers against the side of the young man's neck, though the hole in the center of his forehead indicated it was unnecessary.

"Who are you?" Pearl said from the front of the van. "Are you with the Mercedes?"

Ed slipped the glove back on as he moved around the van's front, where Pearl was pointing her Glock, suppressor attached, at the young man's face. His baseball hat lay in the snow next to him.

He took a deep breath and managed, "I don't...know...anything about...a Mer..." He closed his eyes, mumbling, "Oh, God, it hurts." He looked up at Pearl. "Me and my brother were just playing...with you. I'm sorry...if we scared you. Is Drew...okay?"

Pearl looked at Ed, who had positioned himself behind the wounded young man, deliberately staying out of his line of sight. He shook his head regarding the brother. She frowned, and her eyes flashed anger.

Ed motioned her over to him. As she neared, he nodded toward the blood on her left sleeve, noting the tear across her jacket's shoulder for the first time.

"Got my trapezius," she whispered. "Another graze, I think. Son-of-a-bitch is taking a chunk out of me one shot at a time."

"He's got a semiauto. Anything else?"

"That's all I've seen—and felt. All I was told is that he's..." She grimaced, moving her left arm a little, seeking a position that didn't hurt. "They told me he's an agent, an operator. He does what we do."

Damn, Ed thought, struggling to not let her see his anger. Liam White sent a rookie after an experienced agent. "For whom?"

"Didn't say." She turned toward her truck. "I'm going after him."

Ed knew it was a waste of breath to tell her no. "I'll catch up to you." Pearl nodded.

Ed knelt behind the young man, his eyes noting the blood oozing from the bottom of his sweatshirt. "Where's your phone?"

The man tried to turn to look at him, but Ed quickly stopped him. "Best you stay as you are in case of internal issues."

"I'm sorry," the young man said, grimacing from the pain. "We saw... the blond and thought she was hot. That's all. We...aren't rapists or anything like that. Why did...she shoot me?"

"The man in the Mercedes shot you. Where is your phone?"

The young man's looked toward the open passenger door. "In my jacket. Is my...brother okay?"

Ed stood, retrieved a black jacket from the passenger seat, and pulled a phone from its front pocket. He quickly folded the jacket, knelt behind the young man's head, and gently pulled up the bottom of his sweatshirt. "I'm putting this against your wound. You must put your hand on it and keep pressing to stop the bleeding. Yes, like that. Leave it there until the ambulance comes. You feel like you're going to pass out?" The man shook his head. "Good. What's your password?"

"Titsaregood. One word."

Ed typed it in without reacting, the touch screen feature in Mox's gloves working as advertised. He poked 911 and moved a few steps away. "Man shot on top of the Salmon Bridge overpass over the I-Five freeway," he said when asked if he had a police emergency.

"Salmon Bridge overpass, okay. Is the shooter still there, sir?"

"No. The victim is gut-shot, so please hurry. There is a second shot victim, deceased."

"You said deceased?"

"Yes. Shot."

"What's your name, sir—"

Ed disconnected the phone, moved over to the van, and set it down by the injured man. "The ambulance is on the way. You feel like you're going to pass out?"

The young man shook his head. "Are you with those people?"

"No. I'm on the way to the hospital. My sister has been in an accident. Name's Abram Nelson."

The young man nodded absentmindedly. "No one's telling me about my brother."

Ed patted his shoulder. "I'm sorry, man."

The young man's head jerked to the side as if punched. "Oh, Jesus, no."

"Keep pressure on that wound." He was sobbing now. "Son, don't look at me, just listen. I have to go. But you must keep pressure on that wound."

"Okay."

Chapter 14

Ed didn't like leaving the kid, but he couldn't risk staying with him. The police would come with the ambulance, opening a can of worms that wouldn't end well. The repercussions—exposing Pearl, Cull, The Organization, and himself—would be biblical.

He squinted against the cold air stream coming through the hole in his upper windshield where his rearview mirror used to be and punched in Pearl's cell. "Where are you?" he asked before she said hello.

"If you're just now leaving the overpass, I'm about two miles west. We haven't turned off the road. That guy going to live?"

"Yes. An ambulance and police are on the way. How are you feeling?"

"Right arm is badly trashed. My left arm is not so badly trashed, but the top of my shoulder is on fire."

"You want to shut this down? Answer cryptically."

"I can't. It's essential to finish."

The Organization didn't always tell Ed why a target needed termination, but he knew there was always a good reason. What he knew of Cull, they assigned jobs the same way.

Sometimes, it was because the judicial system had grown weak and impotent; other times because the target had killed before and was about to do it again.

Paul Dillon, another field agent with The Organization, used to say, "Another piece of shit needs flushing down the toilet." Paul was one of the few men he called a friend, and it profoundly hurt when he made one little error and got both femoral arteries severed. The man who did it knew that cutting the leg's femoral could cause the victim to bleed out in minutes. To be sure, the killer severed the femoral in both of his legs.

Killing his friend's killer was one job in which Ed took great pleasure.

Pearl cut into his thoughts. "Okay, we're out of the trees now, and suddenly everything is snow-covered farmland. Visibility is shitty with all the blowing snow. His taillights are about a quarter mile off."

"Hold on," Ed said. "Be back in a moment." He tapped in a number. It rang four times. "One a.m., this better be good."

"The steelhead are running."

A pause, then, "The new angler, okay?" Liam White asked. Ed noticed the lack of empathy in his tone. Maybe it was because he was just pulled from sleep.

"Caught two but functioning. Insists on continuing to fish."

"You think capable?"

"The water is too fast. Might be best to call it a day."

"It's crucial, or I would agree. You angling together?"

"Sort of."

"I'll make it worthwhile."

Ed knew he meant money. "That's not the reason."

"It's definitely critical."

"Okay." Ed disconnected and called Pearl.

"Hi. It's creepy out here," she said, her whisper tight with pain. "Desolate farmland, silent, occasional far-off lights peeking through the snow fog."

"TMI." It was a little late to warn Pearl of too much information on the phone after all the exchanges they had had about Salmon Bridge exit and the overpass. But it was still best to be as cryptic as possible.

"Uh-oh, the lead seems to be slowing."

"You do the same."

The forest on both sides of the two-lane road made for uneven snow coverage on the road before Ed. In some places, it was piled over a foot deep; in other spots, it was bare. It was probably a breeze for Pearl's Dodge Ram, but his sedan had slid twice, though he recovered easily.

A large chunk of snow dropped into his lane about 50 feet ahead. Ed gently slowed to 15 MPH and maneuvered around it. Another clump fell into the oncoming lane near the end of where his headlights reached. He tried to look up to check out the overhanging limbs, but his headlights spread only a few feet off the road. Another chunk fell onto the right shoulder to his front.

Ed's eyes were watering from the rush of freezing air, and he was getting a severe sinus headache. He leaned across the driver's seat and popped open the glove box, hoping to find a tissue or anything to stuff into the windshield's bullet hole. Nothing.

He straightened, squinting at the out-of-place man illuminated in the flat-white light of his headlights. The figure was standing in the oncoming lane about 100 feet away. Ed slowed, leaning over the steering wheel, his eyes watching the man, now almost 75 feet away. Was it the Mercedes driver setting up an ambush? If so, where was Pearl?

Twenty-five feet. Ed slowed to a crawl, ready to accelerate into him if he saw the flash of a weapon. The man was wearing a white bathrobe splattered with blood.

Ed gasped.

It was a hit he had done in Montreal at least 25 years back. He couldn't remember exactly when, but he remembered how. The man, Reginald, something or other, "accidentally" fell from his 18th-floor apartment balcony. Ed remembered that the guy had a strange cry as he dropped, like his favorite childhood cartoon character, Goofy. Whenever Goofy fell off a cliff, which was often, he would go, "Yiiii eee eeee, eee, yaaaa." Ed used to annoy his mother with the yell when he was a child.

The apparition evaporated as Ed neared, but not before it lifted its palm as if to say... What could he possible say?

Ed exhaled, perturbed at himself. "Just stop," he whispered. Then much louder, "Stop!" and goosed the car back up to 30 MPH. He picked up his phone.

"Status," Ed said when Pearl started to answer.

"It's so...dark here," she said as if it were an effort to do so.

"You holding up? If it's too much, we can terminate. There's always tomorrow." Pearl would know he was referring to her wounds. To hell with Liam's insistence, while lying in the warmth of his bed, that the hit was still a go.

"It's like my headlights can barely cut through the dark. No lights at all anywhere, including white and red."

Red meant the Mercedes's taillights, and white the car's headlights. If she can't see them, that means she lost him. Or...

"Ambuscade," Ed said, pronouncing the word 'am-be'skade.

When he and Pearl traveled to Seattle months earlier, they played word games when they weren't doing the getting-to-know-each-other. They kept the challenges job-related. She stumped him with the Japanese word *korosu*, to kill. He got her with the French word for an ambush, *ambuscade*.

"You," he added a few seconds later, hoping she understood that the target might be setting her set up.

"Understood," she said. "There was a Y in the road a quarter mile back. The tire trail went right, and so did I. Now I'm nearing a four-way intersection. I still don't see any lights. No houses. Just dark groves of snow-packed trees. I'm going to stop here."

"If you switch to just your parking lights for a moment, can you see better in the snow fog?"

"Doing it…now. Whoa, that's even creepier. Little trees look like little ghosts, big trees like my worst nightmares. I've stopped about 20 feet short of where the roads cross. I'm turning my lights back on. Okay, I don't see tire tracks in the snow on any of the three roads. No, wait. I think… Let me angle my truck, so I can see better to my left."

Ed listened as her phone relayed the sound of her tires crunching in the snow as she jockeyed into the position she wanted to check. He heard her grunt twice, her wounds probably not liking her arms cranking the steering wheel.

"Okay, there aren't any tracks on the road that continues forward, or to the right…but to the left… There's a jumble of tracks right before the roads cross. One set sort of swings out, and there's another set that I'm betting is backing up to… I'm not sure. It looks like a cluster of vines, but it's hard to tell because they're snow-covered and… Wait, something is…"

"What?" Ed accelerated a little more, though his steering was starting to feel tentative.

"I hear a faint hum of…"

Ed lowered his driver's window but couldn't hear anything other than the wind. The next words he said rapidly. "Honk your horn so I can hear how far away you are."

"It doesn't feel right, Ed," she whispered urgently. "I'm going to back up—"

"Honk your horn."

Ed heard it out his window and over his phone. She was close.

"I see him! The front of his Mercedes is in the brush… He just switched on his headlights, high beam! I can't see—"

BAM BAM

Shots. Loud and clear on the phone and out the window, and it wasn't her weapon.

"Ow ow ow ow ow! Oh God, it hurts! Ed!"

"Keep talking to me!" he shouted, reducing his speed to negotiate a long, snow-covered curve. "Talk—"

"Oh God, he's coming right at me!"

Ed's cheap phone distorted the acceleration of a car engine, abruptly interrupted by a loud smash of metal-on-metal.

"What's going on?" he said, barely controlling his panic. "Talk to me. Are you—"

Ed's car began to slide toward what looked like a ditch on the right side of the road. He dropped the phone onto his lap and used both hands to turn the car into the slide, which sent the phone onto the floor between his feet. He white-knuckled the life out of the steering wheel as the front tires bumped, slid, and groaned the car into a shallow ditch, rocking it to a stop.

Ed could hear a male yelling on the phone, but he couldn't decipher the words. He found the phone with his left foot and trapped it so it wouldn't slide around.

He gently pressed the throttle as he carefully maneuvered his car so that it was length-wise in the ditch, then continued the vehicle's forward momentum, hoping the trench was clear of tree stumps, boulders, and broken beer bottles. There were indistinguishable sounds on the phone for a moment, then silence.

Ed bounced and rattled as he gently turned the steering wheel to ease the vehicle up the small slope until he was again on the road. His headlights illuminated two sets of tire tracks in the accumulating snowfall. The drooping evergreen limbs seemed to be lower than they were minutes earlier.

He retrieved the phone and listened, noting what sounded like the hum of a car, not Pearl's truck, as he had heard each time they spoke in the last hour.

A large clump of snow dropped from a tree high to his left, the newly bare limb snapping back where it had been before the storm, loosening more snow from other limbs to fall.

Another long curve. This time Ed carefully slowed more than last time so as not to lose control and drive over what appeared to be a steep drop-off. The car performed nicely, and a few seconds later, the road straightened. The sedan's headlights revealed Pearl's white Dodge Ram pickup sitting in the intersection, the back driver's side smashed in. His heart sank.

Less than five minutes earlier, she had cried out in pain and called his name.

Ed parked 20 feet away, got out, and extracted his War Club. He slipped the leather cover off the four-inch spur and slipped it into his pocket.

Remaining by his car door, he scanned as much as he could see of the ground under the drooping white trees in all directions, then read the tire tracks in the intersection. The car that hit Pearl came from her driver's side from a clump of low trees and vines. The vehicle must have been secreted deep into it for Pearl not to have seen it until it came directly at her. Even from 20 feet away, he could see a black smear on the rear side of the white truck. The Mercedes was black.

He moved toward the truck's driver's side. Be alive, he thought, hearing a repeat of the shots in his head from a few minutes earlier. "Be alive."

He stopped next to the bed and noted the tire tracks that led up to where it smashed into the pickup; they had been walked on. The car's black transfer paint onto the Dodge, and the doubled-over tire tracks, indicating after the Mercedes hit the truck, it backed up and drove around the front of it. Maybe he didn't want to get out on her side where she could shoot him.

Footprints and what looked like drag marks were made after the car moved. They started below the truck's door and continued around the front. Blood next to the left tire had mixed into the snow. Maybe the threat drove around to the passenger side, found the door locked, and walked back to the driver's side. Did the man assume it was safer to approach the driver's door after looking through the passenger window and finding her debilitated?

"Damn!" he said aloud.

He crept closer. The driver's window was down, but Pearl wasn't behind the wheel. His heart sunk seeing two bullet holes about two inches below the window opening. He looked down at the drag marks in the snow again, then back up at the open window.

Ed again looked around him, the profound silence of the snow-covered forest an eerie entity, adding to his intense unease over the violence that had happened here in the last few minutes and what he was afraid it meant.

He reluctantly straightened from his crouch and looked through the window, hoping, wanting, desperately to find Pearl sprawled out, her eyes happy to see him. But the cab was empty. Her Glock with the attached suppressor lay on the floor in front of the driver's seat.

He backed away from the truck as if it were suddenly venomous. "He's taken Pearl," he whispered. "The son-of-a-bitch has taken her."

Chapter 15

Ed guided his sedan around the pickup as he struggled to control his rage, fear, and dread. All three emotions were dangerous on a job, and he had always managed them well. But he had never had a partner he cared for like a daughter. He should have insisted while on the overpass that Pearl cancel the hit. She was wounded, and while the wounds weren't fatal and were minimally debilitating, one should be in top form for a job, especially when there is an option to wait.

And then there was Liam White's insistence that she finish her assignment. It was "critical," he insisted. I should have insisted at that point, too, Ed thought miserably. I should have stood up for her. White is corporate; Pearl's new and hurt.

He thought of the blood around Pearl's front tire and the drag marks in the snow. They ended where the Mercedes appeared to have parked at the pickup's front right. The traces stopped at what was probably the rear or front passenger door. There was more blood in the snow, probably due to a struggle to get her inside.

Ed had witnessed Pearl's martial arts skills several times. She was a formidable fighter with years of training. She had to be hurt badly to have been taken.

Ed's hands were at ten and two on the steering wheel, white-knuckle gripping it, then splaying his fingers wide, and iron-gripping it again. He was freezing. The hole in the windshield and the open driver's window so he could listen for the Mercedes had chilled his face, punishing him with a deep, throbbing headache behind his left eye.

These things pissed him off even more.

Ed didn't know how far he had driven or for how long when his mind returned to the moment: the tunnel before him formed by his headlights and the white-shroud-covered sentinels that were the trees bordering his way. Where could the Mercedes be going on this lonely road that— He leaned over the steering wheel.

The snow-covered road before him was unmarred by tire tracks.

He slowed to a stop, leaned toward his open side window, and listened. He heard only the movement of wind through the trees. He had to go back in the direction from which he had just come. He studied the width of the road out of his windshield. Snow covered the shoulders, hiding whether the ground was level with the road there or if it dropped into a deep ditch.

Ed had never been a good driver, and it hadn't improved in his upper 70s. He didn't want to back up because he didn't know how far behind him he had lost the trail.

There used to be a former state policeman at Spruce Grove who said the fastest way to turn 180 degrees in the opposite direction was to crank the steering wheel hard as you back up, stop, then turn the steering wheel where you want to go, and hit the throttle. That sounded logical, Ed thought, not knowing if it was and knowing backing wasn't his forte.

He gritted his teeth and did it, nearly driving off each side of the road to an unknown, though likely bumpy, endpoint. Thank you, copper, he thought, not remembering his name. Poor guy choked to death in his room one night.

Ed drove around a long curve, spotting what he had somehow missed when he passed by a few minutes earlier: clumps of disturbed snow and tire tracks turning abruptly toward a low embankment and what appeared to be the edge of a drop-off. Ed's stomach sank.

He stopped short of the tire tracks, patted his side to ensure his War Hammer was in the deep pocket of his overcoat, and opened his door, illuminating Pearl's gun with an attached suppressor on the passenger-side floor.

What…?" he breathed, frowning. Not because he didn't like guns, which was true, but he couldn't remember putting it there. When examining the crash scene, he had seen it in Pearl's truck, but he had no recall of retrieving it and putting it in his car. But then he was quite shocked at discovering she had been abducted.

The slide was back on the Glock, which meant she had probably fired it dry. Hopefully, her rounds found the mark first. If so, they didn't prevent the man from driving. Or maybe, he held his gun on her and made her navigate the car. But with her fighting skills, she would have overpowered him.

But both of Pearl's arms were shot and judging how she screamed after the gunfire at the crash site, she might have more wounds. The thought of the man shooting Pearl clouded his mind with an all-consuming rage. He quickly pushed it aside.

He looked out his windshield at the disturbed snow cluster at the road's edge. It looked fresh. Did they fight inside the car, making the driver lose control and sending them off the road down...

Ed exited the sedan, his mind repeating, don't let Pearl be hurt more; don't let Pearl be hurt more; don't let...

He quickly scanned all 360 degrees around him while at the same time patting his overcoat pocket again to ensure his War Hammer was still in place. He moved over to the tracks and followed them off the road and to the edge of a steep hill.

The white snow-covered trees and the white blanketed downward slope created minimal illumination but enough to see about 60 feet down to where the black Mercedes lay partway on its side, the top resting against a tree trunk, the undercarriage facing up the bank. Chilled-white exhaust flowed from the rear of the car. The front and rear ends were crumpled.

Pearl, he thought as an ice-cold sensation streaked up and down his spine that had nothing to do with the weather.

Without hesitating, he began descending sideways as quickly as possible—lead foot, rear foot, lead foot, rear foot—until his feet went out from under him.

He slid feet first a ways until unexpectantly stopped by a short tree stump mostly hidden under the snow. The sudden impact on the soles of his boots sent a wave of reverberating pain through his legs, pelvis, abdomen, and back, ending at his jaw. He stayed motionless for a moment, mentally scanning his body for injuries. He didn't feel anything new, but the impact reignited the pain in his back from Moxie's sudden weight change when walking her through Dumpy's.

He looked at the Mercedes's exposed undercarriage, now about 15 feet away, and listened for movement inside. Ed heard only the soft purr of the running motor. He quickly scanned the hill to his right, left, and rear, then scooted and slid feet first toward the vehicle's back panel on the passenger side. From this position, he could peek through the back window. If the man were inside and still behind the wheel, he would have to twist around to confront him, giving Ed an extra second to react. He raised himself enough to see the front seat headrests. He didn't see anyone sitting up, but they could both be scrunched below the top of the seats.

Ed maneuvered himself until he was below the rear passenger window. Since the car rested a quarter of the way over on its side, Ed could easily see a bullet hole through the glass. Was that from Pearl's gun? Hopefully, it hit the bastard. Or maybe the man shot through his window at her when she was still in her truck.

Ed waited a full minute, listening for sounds inside the vehicle: breathing, cloth rubbing on the seats, a moan. As before, he heard only the engine. With effort, he worked himself up onto his cold knees and straightened his chilled upper body until his head was below the window. He canted it just enough that only one eye and a little of his forehead were exposed as he peeked through the window.

The car was empty.

He reflexively ducked down by the undercarriage and again surveyed his surroundings on this side of the vehicle. Snow-covered trees on the steady slope continued past the car, the bottom of the hill not visible in the falling snow and darkness. If the tree hadn't stopped the Mercedes's downhill slide, it would have continued down and down. The only footprints above the slope were his, beginning at the edge of the road above to where he now kneeled.

Ed looked up at the roof's edge above the car's passenger door. The light dusting of snow that had fallen since the car had slid down the bank was disturbed there. Since the tilted driver's side rested a foot or two above the ground, the passenger side was the only way out. There were no prints in the snow on this side, so they had to have crawled up on the roof without touching the ground and slid down toward the driver's side, avoiding the tree trunk pressed against the car's top. Ed frowned. Why didn't they take the easy route by dropping on the ground on this passenger side and then walking around to the other side? Maybe the abductor felt they would be more visible than they were going over the roof.

That seemed odd to Ed, but then he wasn't thinking with gunshot wounds in his body.

Still looking above the door, he raised himself a few inches to better see. Fresh blood.

How much of it was Pearl's? He lowered himself back to his knees. The cold had penetrated his ash-colored Canadian Goose Expedition Parka and was doing a number on his cranky knees and hip joints. He forced his discomfort out of his thoughts.

Holding onto the car, he knee-walked around its trunk end and stopped. He listened. If the target was crouched down on the other side, the man had to have heard him moving around the car's rear end no matter how silently Ed tried to skulk. He listened some more. Nothing, not even the sound of breathing. He leaned out just enough to expose one eye.

The top of the car was partially folded around the tree's trunk. Slide marks, spotted with blood, led down the roof to the pine needle-covered bare ground. Three feet out where the tree umbrella no longer shielded the ground, Ed could see footprints in the snow heading off across the slope to a cluster of trees.

But why was there just one set?

He drew his head back and moved over to the passenger side corner of the undercarriage. The snowfall had slowed a little, allowing him to better see the trail the car left as it slid down the hill. About halfway up it and off to the far side of the slide marks was a blue lump in the snow. It moved ever so slightly.

Pearl had been wearing a blue coat.

Had she been thrown from the car? Or maybe she took advantage of the out-of-control slide and leaped from the passenger door. If she had stayed in it all the way down, she would have left footprints to where she lay. Was the man lying in wait for him? Might he be taking advantage of Pearl's position to draw him out in the open? Why didn't the man shoot at him when he was sliding down the hill? Maybe he was still crawling toward the trees, and the falling snow hid him from Ed's line of sight.

Lots of maybes.

The blue lump moved again. This time, Ed recognized Pearl's head as it lifted a little and appeared to be looking his way. He raised his open hand to indicate he saw her, then rotated it palm down. He knew she understood his signal meant to remain in place.

A sudden wind gust blew the snow off the trees next to her, blocking his line of sight to her, but not to the small grove where the footprints ended. There was no indication anyone was there. Maybe the man had kept on going. Or he was lying next to a tree trunk watching everything through a break in the branches.

Tired of the 'maybes,' Ed bent low and began trudging toward Pearl. He couldn't see her in the almost snownado, but he knew he was moving in the right direction. He looked toward the clump of trees again. Hopefully, the man was hurt and not looking his way.

But Ed knew he was. He could feel it.

The wind gust stopped, but the snow on the branches continued drifting down, blocking him from seeing Pearl. Ed's breathing and the soft crunch of his feet was the only sound. The air finally cleared, and he could see her. Her face was smeared with red. She tried to sit up; again, he made the palm gesture to keep her in place.

Bam!

Ed flattened himself in the snow, wishing he was wearing a white coat he would never have in his wardrobe in a million years.

The round struck a tree behind Ed and to his right about 10 feet, sending down white clumps. The target is supposed to be an operator, so how did he miss such an easy shot? The wind picked up again, this time obscuring the view of the clump of trees where the man was likely taking cover. Ed crawled fast, at least as quickly as his freezing body could move. Five feet away, he whispered, "Where are your wounds?"

"I've got...five," Pearl managed, her voice tired, distressed, the side of her face smeared red. Part of her earlobe was missing. "The asshole shot me...five times, Ed. I'm... I'm very tired of him shooting me. It hurts."

Ed crawled next to her and kissed the side of her face. "I had a toothache once that hurt pretty bad."

She pressed her face against his and closed her eyes. "Ed," she whispered. Her skin was cold, her body trembled, and her rapid breathing made a white cloud around both their faces. "Can we...get up to the road?"

"Yes. What's the condition of the target?"

"Bad," Pearl managed. A small glob of blood trickled from one corner of her mouth. She didn't react to it. "I shot him...twice, once in the leg... and once in his upper chest." She wiped her chin with the back of her hand. She didn't look at it. "He's got...something big sticking out of his eye. His right one. A piece of metal or something. The bullet in his chest was from when I popped him through his side window."

"That explains his poor marksmanship." He looked toward the clump of trees again. The falling snow made it hard to see. "Let's start up the hill. Can you stand?" She shook her head. "Crawl on your hands and knees?"

"May...be."

"Try to get up on them. How can I help?"

"Don't...help. I caught a painful one...in my side, by my armpit. I ...need to control...how I move."

"Okay," he said, lightly touching her back.

Her arms shook as she pushed her torso up, followed by one knee, then the other. She looked down at the snow as she put one hand out in front, then scooted one knee forward a little. Again, a stream of blood poured from her mouth, then stopped.

"You're doing good," Ed said, getting up on his hands and knees next to her. "Ready? Hup one, hup two, let's get up this thing."

Ed looked behind them. He hated being the prey. If Pearl was in better shape, he would situate her behind a tree and go after the man. But he needed to get her up the bank and into the warm car. He glanced at her profile, noting the strong determination in her jaw and the intense focus of her eyes. But he could see her pain, too: a spasm in her cheek, trembling arms struggling to hold herself up, and worse, the blood trickling from the corner of her mouth. That was never good.

Bam!

A glob of snow a half dozen feet to their right flew away.

"The blind swordsman is improving," Ed whispered. "I have a War Hammer in my coat pocket," he said, dropping back behind her.

She stopped and, with effort, looked back at him. "Why are you back... there? You ...checking out my butt, Ed?"

"Caught me."

"I... don't want you—" She spat blood into the snow. "Oh God," she said under her breath. Then, "I don't want...you shielding me. I...want you...beside me."

"Keep moving," he said, staying behind her. "We're close."

She did, but painstakingly slow. "His last bullet...at the intersection hurt. Actually, the first four hurt too. But number...five, that one sucked."

"Tell me about one of your college sweethearts."

"What? Now?"

"Yes."

"Okay. Just...one?"

"I have a short attention span."

"Uh, damn. Let me...think. Okay, here's one. I worked at...a little coffee and donut joint three...blocks from the main campus. This guy came in...one night, drunk as a sailor. He...got pissed...because we were out of...ovj magles boz," she slurred, gagged, then hacked a wad of blood into the snow. "Shit!"

"Keep moving, Pearl," Ed encouraged, slapping the bottom of her shoe. "Look, we're less than twenty feet from the road now. So did this guy make a scene?"

"Oh, you know...him! Yes, he....did. He knocked over a...display of cups." She cleared her throat, scooped a handful of snow in her mouth, then spit it out.

"You kick his ass?"

"I...dated him."

Ed laughed.

"I did…for about three months. The…last night…is when I kicked his ass. He tried to…. manhandle me when I wanted to go…meet my girlfriend for a beer. He grabbed my arm…and tried to shove…me down. So I hurt him."

"The beginning of a warrior."

"Not the beginning. I had been training in…karate and muay Thai for…about eight years by then. You know who…John Wayne is?"

"Of course, but I'm surprised you do."

"I do. I love him. What a…man he was. He said…I can't…remember what movie…*The Shootist,* I think it was. He said, 'I won't be insulted. I won't…be laid a hand on. I…'" Pearl dropped to her forearms and coughed violently into the snow. "Ed…I…"

"'I won't be laid a hand on,'" Ed said, patting her calf. "'I don't do these things to other people, and I require the same from them.'"

Pearl laboriously pushed herself up onto her hands. "You know…that one?"

"Clearly."

"Well, isn't…that something. I—"

Bam!

Pearl's arms collapsed under the new weight, burying her face in the snow. She forced her head up. "Ed! Ed! Are you… Talk…to me."

"About what?"

"About…? Damnit, Ed! Are you…hit? Why are you lying on my back?"

He scooted backward off Pearl. "He shot my butt."

"Oh, my God! Can you…still move?"

Ed closed his eyes against the intense burning sensation. One time a guy slammed the end of a steel pipe into his butt cheek, sending him tumbling down a set of stairs. He initially thought the impact cracked his pelvis, but it didn't. Still, the bruised muscles and bones hurt for weeks. This felt more like a blowtorch grooved a path in his cheek. A graze, maybe?

"Yes, I can move," he said, looking behind him. He expected to see the man moving toward him, his gun firing. But he saw only the grove of trees. "Let's keep going. Looks like a dozen more feet. I'll have to drive standing up."

Bam!

"Shitshitshit. You okay, Ed?"

"He missed this time," he managed, his backside freshly burning every time he advanced. "Ten more feet. Good, good. Now eight more."

Two minutes later, they made it up onto the flat ground.

"Keep crawling. The guy might see us if we stand up here. Move around to the driver's side."

"I'm…" Pearl collapsed onto her forearms, "spent. I don't think—"

Ed had been looking down the slope. He thought he saw movement from the clump of trees, but a gust of wind blew snow from the trees blocking his view. "Push yourself back onto your hands," he snapped, moving up along her left side, which was exposed to the hill. If the man shot again and his aim was true, he would catch the round, not Pearl.

"Advance one step. Then advance another. It's all about one more step. We got only about ten more."

She did as he ordered. After two body-trembling steps, she began crying, which Ed could see angered and embarrassed her. But those emotions were fueling her, giving her just enough zip to keep moving. They reached the car but needed to be on the driver's side.

"I got nothing…left, Ed. I'm…I can't…"

"Roll onto your back and hurry," Ed said, looking down the embankment as she struggled to turn over. The snow flurry still blocked him from seeing the trees. He looked back at her. "Okay," he said, placing one knee on each side of Pearl's hips.

"This is hardly…the time, Ed."

"It's an old Army trick," he said, lowering his head near her face. "Wrap your arms around my neck."

"Okay, but you weren't…in the Army."

"John Wayne did this in *The Sands of Iwo Jima*. Now clasp your hands behind my head. Yes, like that."

Ed began to walk on his hands and knees around the car's back end, dragging Pearl underneath him. "If you got any juice in your legs, push with your feet each time I move forward. That's it. Now we're moving."

Two minutes later, they were next to the back door. He crawled off her; her arms dropped heavily in the snow. "I want you in the back seat behind the driver's seat. And lay down."

"K," Pearl managed.

Ed wasn't sure if he could pull Pearl into the backseat from the ground. "You have to get up on your two feet. I'll help you."

"I'll…try," she said, struggling to roll over on her side. She pushed herself up onto her butt as tears streamed down her face. "Your gunshot ass…up for it?"

"No," he said, knee-walking around behind her as a gust of wind smacked his face with snow. He quickly blinked it out of his eyes and inserted his arms under hers from behind, clasping his hands together over her chest. "When we stand, we'll move a step or two to the backdoor." Pearl nodded. "Then I'll—"

Bam-clunk!

The round hit the passenger side of the car. Ed reflexively wrapped his arms around Pearl's head and pulled it down as he scrunched low. He came up enough to look through the car windows. He half expected to see the man coming over the hill, pointing his gun. But he wasn't there. "He's close," Ed whispered, thinking the man was probably bobbing up and down just below the top of the slope.

He considered the trees across the road. They were about 40 feet away; they'd never make it that far. If he pushed Pearl under the car, she would be a sitting duck for an easy kill. The same if she were in the backseat, but at least she would be in place for a fast getaway.

"Ed, can I…lift my head now?"

"Oh, sorry." He removed his arms from shielding her head and inserted them under hers. Then he extracted one, realizing he hadn't opened the door yet. He jockeyed himself and Pearl around to face the opening, his butt against the side of the car, the pressure igniting his wound anew. With some awkward struggle, he opened the door.

"Put your foot in…yes, very good. Now let's get the rest of you in." He grunted, and Pearl cursed until she was seated awkwardly inside, her left leg still out. Ed picked it up and gently set her foot on the floor. "Lie down, and—"

Bam!

Ed reflexively ducked, but not before he saw the bullet hole in the front passenger window. He pushed Pearl onto her side, then eased the door shut, extracted his War Hammer, and duckwalked to the driver's front fender. His butt was in flames, at least it felt like it, but that had to be the least of his concerns now.

Without a visual, he turned up his sense of hearing. He could perceive the wind and the brushing of snow-packed tree limbs moving against one another. And the crunch of a footstep on snow accompanied by a low groan. The threat was hurting too.

Another foot crunch and another and another. He was close now. Ed placed one hand on the ground and bent to look under the car. He could see only one lower leg, the other out of view behind the far rear tire. Could he see Pearl in the backseat?

Ed tapped three times on the side of the sedan to distract him. The man's other foot stepped along the side of the car, followed by the other. They stopped by the front passenger door.

"This is where you die, assholes," the man said. "I see the bitch's weapon with a suppressor on the floor. Slide's open. Empty." If he could see Pearl in the back, he was keeping it to himself.

The wind gusted, then again, harder and louder.

Ed took advantage of the rush of sound and quickly lowered himself onto his belly. He used his forearms to pull and his feet to push until he was all the way under the car with a clear visual of the feet by the passenger door. The man was wearing black running shoes, the white Nike swoosh on their sides. Another gust and Ed scooted farther in.

If he had been 40 years younger, he would have dashed across the road to the trees to draw the man away from the sedan and Pearl. But he wasn't in his 30s, so he would have to make do in a lousy position.

The wind stopped and all was quiet again. No problem, Ed thought. He was within striking range. The undercarriage was too low for Ed to lie on his side, so he would have to fight on his belly. It was awkward and would limit his power, so he had to be target specific.

Ed could hear the man's labored breathing, an indicator of being hurt. Pearl said he had something lodged in his eye.

The feet moved toward the front of the car, then stopped short of rounding the front right fender. He was peeking over the hood, Ed figured. The feet moved again, side-stepping slowly. Ed knew the man was cautiously anticipating him to pop up. The feet moved around the left front fender.

"We're playing ring around the rosy, are we?" The man laughed; the sound forced. Ed envisioned him stretching his neck to see all around the car. "Did you know that rhyme was written in 1665 during London's Great Plague? The words were a little different then."

The man sang as his feet cautiously side-stepped back around the front of the car, returning toward the passenger side. "Ring-a-ring-a-rosies. A pocket full of posies. A-tishoo! A-tishoo! We all fall down." He mock-laughed again, his feet side-stepping past the front right tire. "You see, the roses are a euphemism for deadly rashes. The posies were supposed to be a prevention; the a-tishoos are the sneezing symptoms, and the falling down line is—ha ha— good ol' death. Fitting, eh?"

The guy is nuts, Ed thought, noting that the man's feet were past the passenger door and close enough for Ed to make his move.

He rotated the War Hammer so the four-inch-long dagger-like spur pointed at the threat. An intrusive image of Chick Norris and his deadly spurs popped into his mind. Ed pushed it out of his thoughts and focused on the target.

The man stepped back, too far to reach with the War Hammer. Ed cursed to himself. He waited, his breathing controlled, silent.

The foot shuffled back in range, then turned just enough to present Ed with the Achille's tendon.

"Well, looky here," the man said a big smile in his tone. "The bitch is taking a nap."

Someone in The Organization once told Ed that if you can severely injure an armed person's Achilles tendon, you will activate the acupuncture point that connects to his gun hand. The fingers spring open, and the weapon will drop. Ed thought it was just a theory but hoped it was true.

He whipped the War Club along the surface of the road, out past the edge of the car, and buried the spur deep into the man's Achilles.

"Aaaagh!"

If the man was holding a gun, he didn't drop it.

Ed jerked his hammer back toward himself, ripping the spur through the nerve-rich tendon and out, blood splattering into the snow.

The gun still didn't drop, but this time the man's pain discharged in the form of a godawful shriek. His knees sank into the snow less than two feet from where Ed was retracting his hammer for another blow.

A hand gripping a semi-auto lowered into Ed's view from under the car and canted, the serious end of the barrel pointing at his face. The index finger on the trigger curled before Ed could respond.

The gun didn't fire. The finger yanked the trigger again. Still nothing. That's when Ed saw the reason: The slide was back. The man was out of ammo.

Ed whipped the War Hammer over the snowy road, slamming its four heads into the back of the gun hand.

A jagged bone punched out of the back of the man's hand, and the fingers sprang open, releasing the Glock to plop into the snow next to his knee, his scream once more piercing the muffled wintery wonderland. One knee lifted as if he was going to try to stand, but it thumped back down—on top of the hammerhead.

The man's knee shifted off it. He either didn't realize he had trapped Ed's weapon or maybe he had another plan. If the latter, Ed didn't give him time to act on it as he rotated the War Hammer next to the man's knee, so the long ugly spur was pointed at his kneecap.

Ed jerked the weapon back toward him, the spur catching the man's flesh on the inside of the knee, then gouging a bloody furrow across the bone.

It sounded to Ed that the man had covered his mouth with a cupped hand to stifle his scream, but it was still quite loud. Ed could hear other sounds deep in the man's chest—wheezing, high-pitched grunts, even a growl—all of which gave Ed satisfaction.

But the hitman still needed to be terminated, and quickly.

He thrust the hammer toward the dropped Glock, caught the weapon's trigger guard with the spur, and pulled it under the car, bumping his head on the undercarriage. He ignored the biting pain.

The knees disappeared. Somehow, the man was standing, too far away to hit. The feet shuffled in the snow; a knee came into view, then disappeared. He's having trouble with his balance, Ed thought. Did his knee give out on him?

Ed pushed himself toward the car's rear to get within range of the man's new foot placement. The threat was next to the passenger side's rear door, so Ed had to act before he opened it. The man moved his right foot closer to Ed, the same one with the shredded Achille's tendon. He set it down tentatively, but it flopped partially over to the side, shooting fresh blood from under his pant leg into the snow. He lifted it quickly and made a short forward hop, his support struggling for balance as he fell against the car, joggling the sedan.

A second later, he slowly slid down it until his body thumped into the snow; his legs, one on top of the other, landed three feet from Ed's head. Then the man's face plopped into the snow.

Ed wanted to smash his face to end this, but it would necessitate him scooting a little forward to reach it. But first, he wanted the man to feel some hellish pain, despite his creed to never make a job personal, which he never had. But this time, it was. The man shot Pearl five times and his butt once. It doesn't get more personal than that.

He rotated the hammer and whipped the four steel heads into the man's top shin. The crunch was loud, but the man's scream that pierced the frigid air was deafening. He sure liked to holler, Ed thought, slamming a second bone cruncher into the same nerve-rich shin a couple inches above the first point of impact. Spread the wealth, he thought.

This time the screaming man managed to pull his top leg away, so Ed crunched the shin bones in his other leg a few inches above the ankle.

If he had to guess, the unique hammer was likely leaving four square indents inside a larger square indent in the man's shin bones under his pant legs.

Ed snapped the War Hammer back and started sending another shin-eating blow, but the crying man jerked his second leg away before he could launch. The awkward position of lying on his belly and swinging the hammer was exhausting, and Ed wondered if he could keep it up.

Moving his last leg out of range inadvertently placed the man's head closer to the car's undercarriage, his face still mostly pressed into the snow, his wailing muffled but still loud.

Ed was fine punishing a different target because, based on his experience, more blows to the shins and knees wouldn't hurt to the same extreme as the first ones. The body protects itself when injured repeatedly in the same location by shutting off the pain receptors. That was a more valid concept than the silly acupuncture one.

Anyway, it was time to end this with a lethal hit, but first, Ed needed to know who this guy was. He pushed himself back a couple of feet, so he was at a range to deliver max impact to the head.

"Who do you work for?" Ed asked the buried and crying face. "Hey, lift your face and look at me. I asked who you work for."

The man choked off his sobs and lifted his head. Ed had forgotten that Pearl said he had something protruding from one eye. The large piece of black metal or plastic was in his right eye, the part visible at least three inches long. How much more was deep in his eyeball? Snow clumped around his other eye and mouth and stuck to one cheek. Still, he looked…

"I…" The man shook his head to remove the snow. "I don't know what you mean by the ques—"

"Sam?" Ed said, shocked. "Sam Bartley?"

The man's tear-streaming good eye blinked away the last of the snow then searched for the speaker. "How do you know—" His eye found Ed's face and widened with surprise. "Ed? I… That was you hitting me? I don't understand. Why are you—"

"Aren't you working for Liam White at Cull?"

Sam Bartley grimaced, no doubt feeling his numerous crushed bones. "Yes. I heard you weren't working anymore since The Organization has been wavering after you killed…" He frowned, apparently not remembering the name of Ed's old boss.

"Did Liam put out a hit on you?"

Sam's good eye narrowed. "Seems that way. And I think I know why." He adjusted his position a little, grimacing at the effort. My leg is... goddamn, it hurts. I can't lift it on its own." He reached down with his left uninjured hand.

"Hold it, Sam." The man stopped, looking at Ed fearfully. "You got an ankle gun?"

"I don't, Ed, and that's the truth."

"Slowly then."

Sam grabbed a wad of his trousers, lifted his top leg, and set it down in front of his other.

Ed knew of two other instances when Cull and The Organization put hits on their own people. Cull ordered a female operative to drown when she embezzled four and a half million dollars from their coffers, then threatened to contact CNN when they caught her. The discovery in the books occurred on a Thursday night, Cull confronted her on Friday, she threatened to go to the press that same day, and she "accidentally" drowned that night in her own hot tub.

When a hit was put out on Ed by The Organization, his boss took the job himself. Ed killed him after a long and violent fight.

But why Sam Bartley? Ed had heard he was a good operator, always carried out a job with professionalism, and never left a thread of evidence behind. Liam White had said something to Ed once about Sam being a womanizer and that he had been counseled a couple of times not to let his horndog ways jeopardize a job. Maybe he went too far with that and stepped on some important toes.

"Who's the woman?" Sam asked, nodding his head toward the door above him. "She a rookie?"

Pearl was lying in the backseat directly above Ed, but he had yet to hear her move.

"Not brand new."

"Working with you on this?"

"It was all hers. She called after you shot her."

Sam nodded, caressing the upper thigh of his rear leg. "She hit me once in my side in my driveway, but not before I got her, twice, I think. Her shadow gave her away. Rookie error."

"What happened to your eye?"

"We exchanged rounds on the overpass. One of hers hit my side mirror as I was getting out. I think it's part of the frame. Does it look bad?"

Ed nodded, looking at the eye, watching Sam's hand lightly stroke his blood-soaked hip in his periphery, "Pretty bad, yes. The piece is about four inches long—" Sam's stroking hand dropped behind his hip.

"Show me your empty hand," Ed snapped, but too late because it came back over holding another Glock, the end of the barrel turning toward him.

In a nanosecond, Ed weighed the odds of jamming the gun against Sam's chest or delivering brain damage. With the hammer already in his hand, it would take an extra beat to release his grip on it and then slap his palm against the firearm already pointing at him. Ed went with his gut.

He snapped the four-headed hammer three feet across the snow-covered road, slamming it with sickening force into Sam's already damaged eye socket. The impact drove the long black thing on a quick journey deeper into Sam's eye socket, cranial cavity, and brain.

Ed dropped the War Hammer and slapped his palm against the Glock, pinning it against Sam's heaving chest. He held it there as the man's body bucked, and his head lifted off the ground, then fell back into the snow, all without hollering this time.

He stilled a moment later.

It was then that it occurred to Ed that he could have hit the gun with his War Club. Oh well, it worked out anyway.

Ed pried the weapon from Sam's hand and slipped it into his pants pocket. He retrieved the man's first gun and dropped that into his pocket as well.

"Pearl!" he called out. No answer. The 77-year-old fought his body's desire to close his eyes and let the tension of the last few hours leave his body, but he had to check on her. He called her name again as he scooted toward the driver's side—banging his head on the undercarriage twice—and away from Sam's corpse.

He didn't hear if she replied, but he thought he detected movement from above him. He groaned and squirmed out from under the car and used the driver's door handle to help him stand.

Bright headlights lit up the car. It wasn't until the lights moved away that Ed could see that it was a pickup rounding the curve. He quickly flipped his hood over his head as the red truck slowed, then stopped across from him on the other side of the road. "Need help, partner?" It was dark, but Ed could make out that the man had a full beard.

Ed had parked with the front end of the Chevy sedan angled toward the bank. It was enough to block the truck driver's line of sight to Sam's trashed body stretched out on the passenger side. Ed looked down at the War Hammer in his hand, blood dripping from the spur and the quadruple hammer. He casually moved it behind his leg, then turned partway toward the man, not enough to show his face.

"All's good, thanks." Ed didn't think he could see Pearl in the back. "A small tree limb got caught in my front tire. I got it out." He brushed snow from his coat and pants to underscore that he was working on his car.

The bearded man stretched his head up, looking toward the sedan's back window. "Did I see an arm raise up in the backseat there?" The man moved as if to open his door.

Ed lifted his palm to stop him. Keeping his head diverted by looking in the back window of the sedan, he said, "It's a friend of mine. Got COVID. Tested positive at work for it. Sick as hell. I got it too. You don't want to get close."

"Oh, hell no. Had it twice already. Good luck." His tires spun for a moment, gripped, and he was off.

Ed opened the driver's door, tossed the War Hammer and the man's two Glocks onto the passenger's floor with Pearl's weapon, then pulled open the back door. Pearl was where he had left her, her head on the seat next to the open door. She was looking up at him.

"I…could hear you talking to the target," she managed, her voice thin, breathy.

"I knew him. Sam Bartley. He worked for Liam White."

She frowned. "Works for…Liam? My boss?" Ed nodded. "You…did the guy?"

"Yes, to all three questions. But you softened him up for me. I'll talk to Liam and see what it's all about. Right now, we got to get you to my doctor. I have one who's patched me up for years. She used to contract with The Organization, so she knows what's up. I'll call her on the way."

"Okay," she said, closing her eyes.

Ed slipped off his overcoat and spread it over her body, tucking it under her chin.

"Ed." She was looking up at him.

"Right here."

"I don't…feel good."

"I'm thinking it's because you've been shot five times."

"Funny man."

"I'm shutting the door now. We got to get going."

"Ed?" she said before he could shut it.

"Yo."

"I don't…remember John Wayne complaining…when he got shot."

"Hmm. Interesting. Maybe Johnny had a saying about that." He shut the door.

"Ed?"

He opened the door. "Yo."

"A saying? Like…when he said, 'Life is hard, it's…' I don't…remember the rest of it."

Ed looked in both directions for other Good Samaritans. "'Life is hard; it's harder when you're stupid.'"

Pearl nodded. "Yes." She closed her eyes.

"I'll be back in ten seconds." He shut the door and moved around to the other side of the car, grabbed a wad of Sam's coat, and pulled him over to the edge of the hill. He knew everything in the man's wallet would be under another name with nothing to connect him to his family if he had one, especially not to Liam White and Cull. He glanced down the hill at the Mercedes on its side. His car registration would be false too. Sam wasn't wearing gloves, so his prints would be all over it. No matter. Cull would have created phony fingerprint files leading nowhere.

He placed the sole of his shoe against Sam's hip and pushed him over the edge. It slid a third of the way toward the Mercedes and stopped.

"We're off," he said, slipping behind the wheel. He pulled back onto the snow-covered road.

Chapter 16

"It's me," Ed said into his phone. It was pinned between his shoulder and ear so he could have both hands on the steering wheel to deal with the slick road.

"Who else would call me at this horrid hour?" Dr. Elizabeth Archer said sleepily. "What hurts?"

"I got a minor owie, at least I think it's a minor, and my partner has five; only one's minor, we think."

"Jesus H! Five hits, six, counting yours. You reenact Gettysburg?"

The doc was a Civil War buff. She had worked for The Organization longer than Ed, not as a field agent but as a physician, her practice in Portland. She retired two years back, and she and Ed had remained friends, the two dining together monthly at the Argentine Steak Grill.

During one of their early dinners, after the doc had had three wines, she said, "You've probably been wondering if I have stopped believing in, or if I ever believed in my Hippocratic Oath. My answer is simple. I believe in it with all my being. But I also fervently believe that some sons-of-bitches must be killed for the common good. I've treated a little under two dozen agents over the years—you about, what? Eight times?"

Ed slowed to negotiate a long curve covered with at least four inches of untouched snow. "Not Gettysburg," he said. "But it was a rough game in the snow and ice."

"How bad is your partner; the four that aren't minor?" Doctor Archer asked.

"Real bad."

"I'll prep my workspace. ETA?"

"The snow makes the going slow, but I think under 45 minutes. I have to drop off some tools on the way. Oh, and your car has a hole in the windshield, a rock. It took out your rearview mirror."

"Jesus H, Ed!"

"Sorry."

"Okay, leave the patient here with me, and while I tend to her, you get rid of the car. The VIN, plate, and registration are modified, so they are not traceable. I keep it wiped clean of prints, and I know you always wear gloves. Did the other agent wear gloves in it?"

"No worries, doc," Ed said, not happy that she was talking so freely on the phone.

"Good. But I still don't need a shot-up car in my driveway with blood in it."

Damn, Ed thought. She might as well call me by my name. "Hear you loud and clear. See you shortly." He dropped the phone on the passenger seat before she revealed what he had been doing for 31 years and where he lived. He wondered if she had started drinking again.

Ed couldn't return to the I-5 overpass since it would be teeming with emergency vehicles and press. So he would stay on this backroad until he found an east/west road that would take him west to Highway 99, which ran roughly parallel to the freeway.

Neither his nor Pearl's burner phones had GPS, so Ed was going by the car's compass feature to keep him heading north on the dark, forest-lined, two-lane road. The only light came from his headlights punching through the thick black, reminding him of the headlamps cave explorers wear.

His ghosts were missing an opportunity in the ethereal snowy ambiance to wave at him from the side of the road or stick their bloody heads out from between the trees and go "Boo." He hoped he had seen the last of them.

"Tell me about your first date, Pearl," Ed said over his shoulder. He had been asking her questions every few minutes to keep her awake. Whenever she didn't answer immediately, he would reach blindly over the back seat and nudge her since his rearview mirror was gone.

"He was Chinese," Pearl said weakly. "First...name was Long."

"Long, huh? Is that what attracted you to him?"

"Cute, Ed. He was a very...nice boy. He...lived a traditional Chinese lifestyle."

Ed waited for her to continue. She didn't. "Pearl?"

"Yeah," she said groggily. "I need sleep—"

"No, you don't. Where did you go on your date?"

"Who?"

"You and the Long guy."

"Oh, to Olive Garden. His...parents came along." Ed chuckled. "They would...Oh, God, it hurts, Ed. It hurts so bad."

"His parents would do what?"

"Their…English was bad… So the three of them would talk in Chinese, all…the while looking at me. Louie, that was Long's…American name… would translate. He'd say, 'My mother wants to know…what you weigh.' And, 'My mother wants to know how much money my father has.'"

Silence. Then quiet weeping. As long as she was awake, Ed thought.

He carefully rounded a tight curve, revealing an intersection with traffic control lights 50 yards ahead. A snowplow passed through going east, and a Franz Bakery truck went west. Ed looked for a street sign as he slowed for the red light. ANCHORAGE BOULEVARD. Ed knew it crossed 99.

The weeping had stopped shortly after he turned left on Anchorage. "It won't be long, Pearl. Doc Archer has many years of experience patching up agents. She was also a physician on the USS Repose Hospital Ship in DaNang Harbor during the Vietnam War."

"K."

"Did you end up dating Long, despite his annoying parents?"

"No. No chemistry."

Silence, then, "Ed?"

"Pearrrrrl?"

"I was going…to say something nice, but you're…being smarty."

Ed smiled. "Tell me."

She cleared her throat, coughed a little, then violently. Ed lifted himself and turned enough to see her leaning off the seat and spitting up on the floor. If she was gagging and gasping, she was alive, he thought.

He hung a right turn on Highway 99 and proceeded north. The streets were cleared on the main thoroughfare, and the businesses, though closed at this late hour, were lit, a welcome sight from the dark, dense woods they had been in.

He looked down at the cache of weapons on the passenger's floor. Sam's two Glocks, Pearl's with the attached sound suppressor, and his War Hammer wet with blood and eye goo. The Organization and Cull used "gun wranglers" to dispose of agents' weapons after a job. The term was taken from the movie business and referred to those responsible for firearms used by actors on sets. Ed had never used the wrangler assigned to his area because he had never used guns.

"Ed?" Her voice was strained, tight.

"How are you doing, sweetie?"

"Talk…to me, please."

"Sure. A half block in front of us is a boarded-up service station, the pumps removed." Ed guided the car onto the cracked cement lot and stopped, leaving the car and heater running. He twisted around enough to see Pearl's face. She was scrunched into the corner, her eyes closed, her breathing rapid. She opened one partially.

"You're supposed…to be talking to me, Ed."

"It doesn't look like you put on makeup this morning," he said.

"Hil-fucking-arious."

"Okay, I need two minutes, then we'll be on our way again." She closed her eyes and nodded almost imperceptibly. "Stay awake."

He climbed out, limped around the front to the passenger door, and opened it. The interior ceiling illuminated the backseat, revealing Pearl's face better. Pale, bloodless, except for the blood on her lips. He had to hurry.

"Ed…are you there?"

"Yes, ma'am. I'm stripping your weapon, removing the suppressor, springs, guide rod, slide, barrel, and frame. Now I'm doing the same with Sam's empty Glock 17. I'm putting them all into a neat pile. Whoops, the springs want to escape under the seat. So I'm going to set my War Hammer between the seat's substructures and the parts to prevent them from rolling out of sight."

Ed pocketed the smaller Glock.

As he started to close the door, he noticed a street drain at the side of the entrance to the station. "I'm going to donate the two springs to a drain. Be back in a sec." He carried the springs over to it and dropped them through the slots.

"Another quick stop, Pearl," Ed said once they were rolling again. "Up here at Douglas Bridge is a primo spot."

Pearl coughed a couple of times, the sound wet and painful. He turned enough to see her spit on the floor again. She plopped her head against the seat back with a groan and closed her eyes.

"When I was a teenager," Ed began, "I had a buddy who lived by Douglas River, a short walk to the bridge. He said the river often flooded because of snowmelt. It was 75 feet deep in the summer and had consumed not just a few cars and trucks after their DUI drivers crashed through the guardrails that preceded the bridge and sunk, the drunks drowning long before their vehicles ever touched bottom. After four snowstorms this fall and winter, it will be even deeper now."

"Okay," Pearl managed.

It was 3:10 a.m., and the snow and wind were increasing again, reducing traffic to three other cars in the last 10 minutes. DOUGLAS BRIDGE, the sign announced. "We're here." Ed slowed and guided the sedan up the slope onto the bridge. "Talk to me, partner."

"I have to go to the bathroom."

"What? No."

"Just...bull shitting you."

Ed shook his head in mock disgust, "Anyway, no traffic coming our way from the front and not a lone vehicle behind us." He stopped at the midpoint across the bridge and reached down to the pile of parts on the passenger side floor. "I'm getting a guide rod, two frames, and one slide to donate to the river. Don't run off."

He got out, walked quickly to the other side of the narrow bridge, and looked down at the river, pleased to see it roaring past so fast. He chucked one frame as far as he could toward the right side of the river and tossed the remaining slide and the second frame toward the left, but several feet short of the first one. He dropped one guide rod straight down.

Quickly back at the car, he retrieved the slide and threw it as far as possible into the river on that side of the bridge, likewise, with the last guide rod.

"Done here," Ed said, looking around the driver's seat at Pearl before getting in. She was still sitting with her head back, eyes closed.

"Are you thinking about what a great guy I am?"

She nodded, but just barely.

"One more stop along the river. Getting rid of this evidence is adding less than ten minutes of travel time to the doc's place, but it must be done. The police are likelier to stop us in this weather since traffic is almost nonexistent, especially since there were killings not many miles away. So it's important to get rid of it."

He guided the car down the slope and hung a right at the bottom onto a farm road that paralleled the water. "We're in luck; the road's plowed. When I hung out with my friend around here, one of the farmers had a road plow and kept the road passable during winter storms. I'm sure he's passed on, so maybe one of the sons got the farm and the plowing job. Anyway, another inch has fallen since it was scraped, but we can handle it."

"We?" Pearl breathed. "I'm pretty busy...hurting right now."

A moment ago, she could barely nod; now, she was wisecracking. That's a good sign. Ed hoped.

He drove about a mile, stopped at a pullout he remembered from all the years back, and got out. "Be back in a sec," he said before closing the door.

He couldn't remember how far the river was from the road, but it sounded like a few yards. He hurried as best he could through the trees without falling—the illumination from the snow poorly lit the way—eventually arriving at the place where many submerged fallen trees had been. Fishermen hated the spot because they lost so much gear, but his friend knew exactly where to lower their lines to catch big trout and not get snagged. What little he could make out of the river, submerged logs still jammed up against the bank.

He tossed one of the gun barrels halfway out, successfully sinking it next to a partially submerged log. He made his way up the river 10 yards and tossed out the other barrel. Another 10 yards, and he got rid of the suppressor.

Ed slipped and stumbled back to where he emerged from the trees and worked his way back to the car. Pearl had scooted herself up. She was crying as he got in.

"Where were you?" she blared with surprising strength, given her condition. "I thought...you left me."

"Never. I got rid of all the gun parts. It wouldn't look good if the police stopped us—" He glanced down at the passenger floor. The War Hammer! He could leave it since it was just a hammer of sorts. But it was wet with blood and eye gunk. "I'll be back in one minute, and then we'll get you to the doc."

"Ed...listen." He twisted around. She had pressed her head and shoulders into the corner, her eyes unfocused.

"Let me open the door and situate you more comfortably."

"No, I don't need... Just listen."

"Okay."

"You...you have been many things to me. Teacher, friend...father."

"Pearl, let me get rid of this War—"

"When I say...father...I mean it. It's—" She coughed violently, spraying blood droplets on his coat that bunched up on his lap. He reached back and touched her knee, now jammed against the back seat. She took his hand, taking a moment to find her breath.

"Hold on," he said, slipping his hand out of her grip. Ed slid into the backseat and scooted close to her. He wiped the blood from her mouth with the back of his hand, then pulled his coat up to cover her chest. "I really think you need to rest—"

She reached up and took his hand, wrapping hers around it. "Before, I wanted you to talk to me... Now, you listen...to me."

"Okay," he said, looking into her eyes. There was something... He didn't want to hear what she had to say. "Your hand is cold, Pearl. Let me crank up the heat and—"

"Stay, Ed." She took a deep breath and released, her face reflecting the pain it caused her. "Tell me what I...was trying to do...for Cull... Was it right? Morally...right?"

It was the same question he had wrestled with for years, and every time, his self-answer—that he was doing moral work for the greater good—satisfied him. But of late, there has been a nag in the back of his mind that countered his justification with, *Just because you think it doesn't mean it's true.* But that was *his* counter. Pearl would have to listen to arguments in her own heart.

"If it wasn't right, Pearl, I wouldn't have done it for so long. Every job I have done saved lives. And it served as closure for others affected by the target's crimes against them. You're doing a righteous job. Your heart is in the right place. There is no better work than serving others and giving them peace of mind. You're morally right and ethically right."

Pearl's thumb rubbed his hand as she digested his words. Then, "'Did a righteous job.' Past tense."

"Don't talk that way, Pearl. "Let's get moving. We're about twenty-five minutes from—"

"You have my mother's address...phone num... She knows what...I was...doing. Everything in my wallet...is false."

"You will see her—"

Pearl's grip weakened. "I love you as a father, Ed. And a wonderful... friend. I'm so glad...you came into my...life."

Ed's face suddenly burned, and his eyes teared. "And I'm glad—"

Pearl pressed her head back against the seat and inhaled sharply. "Ed..."

The muscles around her mouth tightened and then relaxed as a long breath escaped her partially open mouth.

Her lifeless eyes looked at him.

"Noooooo," Ed whispered.

Chapter 17

Ed had been driving mindlessly for about ten minutes when he realized he was doing 70 MPH on a slick highway in a posted 40 without any idea where he was going. Pearl was lying down in the backseat where he had left her after performing CPR. He covered her with his overcoat afterward, tucking it around her neck and closing her eyes. Anyone glancing in the back windows would only see a sleeping woman at 4 a.m.

He had climbed out of the backseat, his arms and legs trembling, took a few deep breaths, and then pushed his way through the brush again to the river. He tossed the War Hammer out into the deep. The gun pieces and hammer would be found someday, but by then, they should be rusted and look of no consequence. Dumping them in the river wasn't the best way to deal with weapon parts. Still, he had to get rid of them quickly since he was only a few minutes away from two crime scenes in which there were fatally shot bodies and a third scene where Pearl's truck had been smashed and blood left in the snow.

The small Glock still sat heavily in his pants pocket.

"You're not here yet," Dr. Ellen Archer answered instead of saying hello.

"She…"

"Damn, damn, damn," the doctor said softly. "I'm sorry, my old friend."

"This one hurts bad, doc."

"I can't imagine. Do what you must do, then call me in a couple days, and I'll buy you dinner."

Ed nodded, unaware that he hadn't responded verbally. He disconnected and pocketed the phone, glad she had been cryptic this time. Ed's heart hurt so much that he'd forgotten about getting shot in the butt. And so had Dr. Archer.

He pointed the car in the direction of St. Thomas Hospital in Northwest Portland, driving cautiously to not draw the attention of the police.

The hospital occupied about four city blocks on the edge of a crime-rich area where killings were part of the ambiance. Cameras were everywhere on the hospital grounds, so he couldn't just drive up to the emergency entrance and leave the car. He would have to drop it in the neighborhood.

He kept asking himself if this moment was the culmination of his life's work. All these years have led to right now: driving the body of a young woman close to a hospital where he would leave her in the shadows of a side street on a grave-cold night so he could get away.

He shook his head. Maybe it was time I got caught. What a finale that would make: handcuffed and sitting in the back of a police car.

No. Hollywood would run with his story as they have so many mass murderers, making him a hero, his name a punchline. Little kids would dress like him on Halloween, college psychology professors would lecture about what was inside his head, and the students would debate whether he was a brutal, sadistic killer, a violent vigilante, or a hero of the people.

Lake Street was one block east of the hospital and marked with numerous signs that read NO PARKING and RESERVED FOR POLICE AND OTHER EMERGENCY VEHICLES. Vandals had knocked out the streetlights on both ends, leaving the street in darkness, except for some dull illumination made by the snow. Perfect, Ed thought, pulling in behind what looked like an unmarked police car. Some cops might think his vehicle is just another unmarked. But those who take a second look will see the hole in the windshield. And Pearl in the backseat. That was what he hoped, but only when he was far away.

Ed reached over the seat and grasped the sleeve of his overcoat. He had initially tucked it under her chin when she had been shaking so hard. She coughed blood on it several times, but he hoped the dark material and the night would make the spray invisible to the casual observer at four a.m.

"I'm so sorry, sweetie," he said as he pulled the overcoat over the seat back. "Sorry sorry sorry sor—"

He wept for a moment, despite knowing that the longer he stayed with the car, the greater the chance of another police car parking on the street. Finally, he choked it off. He reached back and touched Pearl's hand. Cold. "Goodbye," he whispered. He started to get out, stopped, and turned back to her. "I'm so sorry," he whispered. "I should have talked you out of the job the first time we met. Should, should, should…"

He turned back to face the front and wiped his cheeks. He checked the street and sidewalk to his front, behind him in the side mirror, and across the street. Clear. He got out, slipped on his overcoat, locked the car, and stepped over to the flattened tracks made by passing cars. He scooted his feet along the packed snow to minimize his shoe marks until he reached the intersection. He crossed the street and proceeded down another made dark by streetlight vandals.

Ed calculated that he had about a four-mile trek to Spruce Grove, hard for a young man in the bitter cold and snow that sometimes came down sideways in the intermittent gales. But for a 77-year-old man... Focusing on how tough the journey was only made it tougher. Got to stay positive. He scrunched his head into his coat collar as he crossed the next intersection. A wave of guilt washed over him for taking his coat from Pearl, though he knew he wouldn't survive the long walk without it.

A quote incongruously popped into his head from somewhere. "It's not the journey or the destination. It's who you travel it with."

Like Florence. Moxie. Pearl.

Pearl had been so excited when she accompanied him on a hit not long after they met. Ed shook his head, realizing it had only been a few months ago. He had been excited, too, when he first began so many years ago. Experience, especially those jobs where he was nearly killed or caught, cooled his excitement, eventually eliminating it and replacing it with serious and methodical professionalism. In the few months since he had seen her this time, he could detect a change beginning to wash over her.

He could feel the weight of the Glock 9mm in his pants pocket. Why didn't he toss it into the river when he had a chance?

Ed never had a personal grudge against any of his targets because he didn't know them. He even dressed nicely for their last day alive because it showed respect to them and his professionalism on the job.

Some clients ordered special methods, such as using a saw and various techniques reminiscent of the medieval ages. A few times, the assignment was to terminate slowly. He was fine with special requests, but Ed always refused a job where the client wanted the hit done with a firearm. He was intensely bothered by news stories of drive-by shootings, murder/suicide cases, nut job shooters in malls and workplaces, and, what must be satanic-driven, mass school shootings. As a true American patriot, these things made him nauseous and shamed by what the country had become. As such, he had long ago promised himself never to use a firearm on the job, and except for twice when he was a rookie, he never has.

Just as he was about to walk past a large pickup—a Ford, Pearl's was a Dodge Ram—Ed spotted a police car heading in his direction. He remained by the passenger's door, bent enough so his head couldn't be seen through the door's window. The police car crept by, slowed, then stopped about 20 feet from the truck's rear in the middle of the snow-covered road. The officer activated his spotlight and flashed it between two houses on the other side of the street. The light extinguished, and the car moved on, stopping once more at the end of the block to shine the spot across the intersection. Ed waited until the police vehicle turned before he commenced walking.

———

Ed stepped off the elevator and stopped, not knowing why. It was too early to hear the usual sounds from the ten apartments he shared on this sixth-floor wing—TVs, radios, arguments. He had the hallway and its silence to himself.

He turned toward the large window to his right.

The morning sun struggled but would no doubt fail to show itself from behind the menacing, heavy-hanging, gray snow clouds. He moved over to the window and looked at the north grounds, deep with snow, the trees burdened with it, broken branches lying on the ground under some of them. Beyond the trees and hidden behind the ceiling of clouds sat the mighty volcano Mt. St. Helens no doubt feet-deep with fresh snow. The mountain blew its top off in 1980, obliterating an entire lake at its base, laying down flat acres upon acres of tall trees, killing unfortunate humans and wildlife, and blanketing Portland in gray ash for days. Ed thought it would happen again, and maybe it wouldn't stop next time.

He looked down six floors at the chicken coop. He had no intentions of looking…or maybe he did. Why else did he walk over to the window? Either way, he was doing it now.

Light from the kitchen cast a yellowish hue through the cyclone fence surrounding it, the snow-cleared ground, and the little houses that sheltered the birds from the weather. The custodian must have swept the snow out of the pen.

Strange. Ed could see a half circle of… He moved a little to his left to see around the glare caused by the hall lighting. Not a half; it was a full circle of chickens, about a dozen surrounding something black. Ed used his sleeve to wipe his breath fog from the glass.

The black thing was Chick Norris.

The rooster lay motionless, crumpled. One wing looked torn part way off, and the feathered body that had been a rich black lay splashed with red, as well as the ground and the random patches of snow. There were feathers all about, black ones. It had been a massacre.

From stillness, the circle of chickens moved as one body, first leaning to the left, then right, and back to the left again, all in perfect unison.

Ed thought of how Chick Norris had looked up at him after he killed the rat with its deadly spur. Would the chickens look up at—

He took a large step back from the window.

He had often flashed on that killing moment. Sometimes he was convinced he imagined the rooster looking up at him, a symptom of his memory failing him and filling in the gaps with fantasy. Other times, he knew it happened, which was as frightening as imagining it, more so. But was there a third option? Could the rooster have been showing him what was in his future?

I need to talk to a shrink, Ed thought, though not seriously considering it. Not because the psychiatrist-patient confidentiality would last about 10 minutes before the shrink dialed 911. It was because Chick Norris really had seen Ed's future. Or set it in motion.

The rooster had thumped the rat a few times with his feet before spearing his vicious spur through the rodent's neck, instantly terminating its life. Last night, Ed retrieved his War Hammer to take with him to help Pearl. When he used it, his offense was the opposite of the rooster's, a sort of mirror image. Ed used his weapon's steel spur first to soften the Cull hitman before finishing him with a deadly thump with the four-headed hammer side.

He took another large step back from the plate glass window. No, he thought to himself. I'm not going to look down there and see all those goddamn chickens turn in perfect synchronization to look up at me.

He hurried down the hall, stopping long enough to place his palm on Mox's door, then moved on to his apartment.

He leaned back heavily against his kitchen counter, sending a pen and opened bills cascading to the floor. He lifted his palms to his face and tried to cry, needing to, but the tears wouldn't come.

He thought about the rooster again.

For a second, back at the window, when it occurred to him that the dead black thing in the center of the circle of chickens was Chick Norris, he thought about going down to the pen and looking at him. But he didn't because... Because he knew the black-feathered rat killer would be staring at him, his dead eyes telling him silently that he knew he had wounded his prey today with the War Hammer's iron spur and then killed him with the four-headed end.

"But," the rooster's eyes would convey sagely, "we can't win forever. Look at me? This is how we end."

Ed laughed at that, a chuckle at first, then an all-out horselaugh. A moment later, the tears came and continued to flow for a few minutes. When they finally ceased, he filled a glass of water from the tap, drank, then extracted his phone from his pocket.

On the second ring: "I recognize the number," Liam White said. "How did it go last—"

"She's gone," Ed interrupted.

Seconds of ragged breathing, then, "Damn."

"The target worked for you." A statement.

"Yes." Ed heard not an iota of emotion in the two words.

"Did she know that?"

"No. Just that he was in the business. I didn't tell for whom."

"Why not?"

"My second in command thought it would be a good test for her, her first big challenge. I concurred."

Ed struggled to keep his rage out of his voice, though his empty hand was clenching, relaxing, and clenching again. "She had done a few relatively easy jobs before this; you knew that, right?"

"Of course."

"And still you sent her. Trial by fire? Was that your thinking?"

"Yes."

"What did the target do to warrant the job?"

"Come on."

"You sent a rookie up against an experienced employee."

"I'm sorry she failed," Lian said flatly.

"Stand by," Ed said, then lowered the phone, letting his phone hand hang at his side while he collected himself. He lifted it back to his mouth. "Liam?"

"Don't say names on this pho—"

"Liam White. You're next. See you soon." Ed clicked off and dropped the phone on his counter.

Epilogue

Ed had always been comfortable with his own company. He liked people, especially women, but he was just fine being alone with himself, even for long periods. There had been times in his life when he went for days without talking to anyone other than ordering a coffee from a barista or a stack of pancakes at his favorite diner. He believed he was a prime example of the expression: being alone didn't mean being lonely.

He pushed down on the handle at the side of his recliner to lean back and raise the footrest. With visibility through the ice rain-coated glass door at about 20 percent, he could barely see the snow-topped spruce trees in the front yard. Considering how hard the wind gusts sent the clicking ice rain against the door, he had about 10 minutes left of visibility.

The clicking was like seconds ticking by on an old clock, each one a reminder that time marches on. And the gusts carrying the frozen rain across his balcony were like sharp exhalations of passing time's final breaths. Ed had never been bothered by being alone, but this time it felt…empty. Gloomy. Dark.

He moved his left thigh just enough to slip his hand between it and the chair's arm. He retrieved the Glock 9mm from his pants pocket with his index finger and thumb and placed it gently into his right palm.

He looked down at it, felt its weight, noted the loaded magazine protruding a little, and rubbed his thumb along the barrel.

The two times he used a firearm in his rookie period, the incidents were lead stories on the 5 o'clock news and the front page of the daily newspaper. Were some twisted people encouraged by the stories, turned on by them? Did Hollywood get movie ideas from them? Did a bullied school kid consider getting a gun and delivering some payback in his classroom? Did any of them follow through?

It was because of those unanswerable questions that he never used one again. Some people would vehemently argue against his reasoning, but he didn't care. It was his philosophy, one that he has held near and dear for over 30 years.

Last night a gun took Pearl's life. He looked down at the Glock in his palm. He didn't think it was this one, but Sam was packing it when he used his other weapon on her. Ed smelled the end of the barrel, recently fired. So at least one of the five rounds that hit Pearl came from this one. Maybe it happened when his other Glock ran out of rounds, and he couldn't stop to reload, so he used this to shoot at her. Or Sam could have used it to shoot at Pearl and him struggling up the embankment, the round ripping a path across his butt cheek. The thought made his wound burn and the bandage he had applied to himself to feel bulky and irritating.

Ed squeezed his eyes shut, but tears emerged from them despite his effort to hold them in. When his right hand holding the weapon began to tremble, he used his thumb to pin the gun against his palm so it wouldn't fall. Then just as quickly, he no longer wanted to touch it, to feel it. He deliberately tilted his palm enough to slip the gun off and onto his lap. He wiped his hand on the end of the chair's armrest as if wiping off something foul.

He squeezed the chair arms, digging his fingers into them. He relaxed them and dug into them harder, wanting to punch through the leather. He realized he was panting as if jogging up steep stairs. He focused on getting control of his breathing, but it didn't work this time; it accelerated more.

Moving images rolled across his mind.

A tree. Straddling a high limb. Reaching for the limb above, missing it. His sudden loss of balance. Falling 15 feet onto exposed thick roots, landing first on his wrist—the bone's sharp crack loud—then his side, bruising his ribs.

He thought of Mrs. Ells, his mother's friend. At 13, Ed was confused about how she looked at him whenever her son was distracted. She would look at his crotch for a long moment, then her eyes would slither, like a wet tongue, up to his face. One rainy afternoon when Ed's friend had gone fishing with his dad, Mrs. Ells invited him in for a Pepsi. He hadn't finished it when she began directing his first awkward movements. She was an amazing teacher, and he was a great student. She would be the one he would compare other women against for a dozen years.

Ed thought of the first man he killed and the disappointment in the target's eyes as he comprehended that his life was oozing out of him. The eyes didn't accuse Ed, beg him for help, or tear. They seemed to accept his death as if he had been expecting it. Ed's training coach, he couldn't remember the man's name, pronounced afterward, "Very good. You're a natural."

His eighteenth job was the one that haunted him the most. The order was to hit the target in the man's home garage in San Francisco. The wife would be at work, and their two little boys would be in school. The client's special request was to strangle him. The Organization charged more for special orders, and the field agent's job was to do them no matter how difficult the client's demand was. This one was easy enough: strangle him with a garrote.

Ed twisted the two hanging light bulbs off in the old garage and slipped out to wait along the side of the unattached structure. The rain was coming down hard, the wind slapping it into his face, so he had to strain to hear the man close his backdoor and open the small one to his garage. The target cursed and said what sounded like, "The damn lights are out in here again." He said something else, but Ed couldn't make it out. He heard the car door shut twice.

Ed quickly slipped through the small side door, noting that the man's driver's window was down. He ignored the target's startled expression as he looped the wire garrot around his neck. The man gagged, "Don't hur—" before the thin wire sliced through his carotid arteries, freeing the oxygenated blood flowing to his brain to stream down his business suit.

It wasn't until the man dropped over to his right that Ed saw the little boy, eight or nine-year-old, sitting in the corner of the backseat, his eyes terrified, his mouth open in a silent scream.

Ed refused work from The Organization for several months after that, spending half a year doing nothing but basking in the sun in Cancun. He did everything he could to bury the memory. After a couple of weeks, Ed was doing as well as expected. But then two morbidly overweight women sprawled on lawn chairs close enough to hear them talking as he lay with his eyes closed.

They discussed a magazine article about a little boy who had witnessed his father's brutal murder in California. While untouched by the killer, the incident left the child with a profound stutter. The writer interviewed a psychologist unrelated to the case and asked him about someone traumatized by witnessing horrific violence perpetrated against a loved one and if the resultant damage ever goes away. The psychologist said there were no absolutes about how someone reacts when exposed to horror and how they respond to treatment in its wake. This unknown was especially true when the witness was a highly impressionable child. Worst case scenario, the doctor said, the young one might have long-term problems.

Ed kept telling himself as he hurried to his room that it wasn't the same child. Nonetheless, he stayed drunk for two days and nights in the hotel bar. A first for him, ever.

He shivered slightly in his recliner and pushed the memory back into the same dark place that contained so many others. The frozen glass door now prevented his view of the tops of the spruce trees. No matter because another moving imaged crossed behind his eyes of a sunny spring day here at Spruce Grove several months ago.

As he often did, he was helping Carlos, the 60-year-old head gardener in the vast backyard. He and Ed had become friends over the last three years. Ed often worked with the man in the huge garden that supplemented fresh food for the cafeteria, fertilizing the large yard front and back, trimming bushes and trees, and planting new ones.

A dozen spruce trees forested the large backyard, most towering 60 to 80 feet. Almost centered among the green skyscrapers stood a two-foot infant spruce Ed and Carlos planted in April. Afterward, they sat on the grass and contemplated it as the warm July sun soothed their decades-old bodies. Carlos broke the silence, saying softly, "On the last day of the world, Ed, I want to plant a tree."

"A fine goal," Ed said, his eyes focused on the sapling's bright green needles. "You love what you're doing, my friend."

Carlos nodded. "Trees calm my soul. Heal it too, at least a little." He turned to look at Ed. "I think your soul is calmed by being out here too. Is that why you like to help me dig and plant and trim?"

"Nah, it's your charm, Carlos. I'm smitten."

"You can't bullshit a bullshitter, you know?"

"I know," Ed said, looking at the man. He held Carlos's eyes for only a moment, long enough to feel something pass between them, a kind of *knowing*. He had sensed it before, but he understood what it was this time. Ed had often felt his eyes on him as they toiled in the yard together. Initially, he thought Carlos was simply double-checking his work, but after a while, Ed's gut told him that the man was debating the accuracy of what he saw through Ed's windows to his soul.

Carlos spoke first, his voice a whisper. "Your eyes, my friend, have been there."

Ed studied Carlos's face for a long moment as his mind asked if he was going to try to kill him, or he was asking himself, as Ed was, are we two kindred spirits who have found one another in a garden. "'Been there?'" He asked.

Carlos took two steps toward Ed and stopped, his head slightly canted to the side. "You know the meaning of the words," he stated.

"They mean the soul has been hurt forever. I've seen it in your eyes too." Carlos's nod was slight, but Ed saw it. "Where did you work?" Ed asked, letting the vagueness of the question hang in the air.

"In Mexico. Not for the cartel," Carlos said quickly as if reading Ed's first thought. "But their leaders were often my assignment."

Ed nodded his understanding that "assignment" and "target" meant the same thing.

"And you?"

"In this country," Ed said.

Neither spoke for several minutes, each looking at the little tree. Ed watched him out of his periphery, wondering why he so freely confirmed Carlos's perceptions.

Ed remembered observing a man in the cafeteria a few days after he moved into Spruce Grove. Ed never saw him sitting with anyone as he ate his meals or sat in the TV room. His body seemed to sag as if exhausted from carrying an enormous burden. But his eyes told a story of sadness, pain, horror, and death. Just out of curiosity, Ed sat in the TV room one afternoon in a chair near him. The TV was off, and they had the place to themselves. The man nodded at him, returned to his paperback, then looked back at Ed, frowning as he looked deep into his face.

"I was with the Marines," the man said, "wounded my tenth month halfway up Hill Eight Eighty-One near Khe Sanh in northwestern Quang Tri Province in Vietnam. I lost all my buddies. But I got sixteen of the mutha fuckin' Charlies." He looked at Ed for a moment, then, "You?"

"Thanks for your service," Ed said, thinking it sounded lame. "I didn't serve. I couldn't pass the physical. Bad lower back."

The grizzled old timer leaned forward, his clear, intense eyes boring into Ed's. "Bullshit. You were over there; I can see it in you." He leaned back. "You have seen the light in the enemy's eyes go out right in front of you as they died from your doing."

"You're wrong," Ed said, standing. He avoided the man after that. Four months later, the veteran died alone in that same chair.

Carlos saw something in Ed's eyes, and Ed saw something in his friend's eyes. He couldn't say what it was and doubted Carlos could either.

In Ed's 30-plus years working for The Organization, only Pearl and Florence knew what he did. Of course, Pearl came into his life already knowing. Now Carlos knew, though vaguely.

Ed and the gardener didn't say anything more about it that day or in those that followed.

After their mutual acknowledgment, Carlos had stretched out on the soft, fragrant grass, braced by his elbows, his head tilted back, eyes closed as if to let the gentle breeze wash over his face. Ed remained cross-legged, chewing on a piece of grass and looking at the little spruce. When Ed spoke again, his voice was low, contemplative.

"I will never sit in the shade of this great tree."

The most powerful wind gust of the morning rattled the frozen door, bringing Ed back to his room and recliner. He placed his hand on the Glock so it wouldn't fall off his lap and adjusted himself in his chair.

More memories flashed across his mind.

The sweet sound of Florence's laugh when he said something silly or, more often, when she got the best of him at "breaking balls," as she liked to call their mutual teasing. She said she was good at it because she grew up in the Bronx with four brothers.

The terrified little boy's silent scream from the backseat seconds after he witnessed his father's violent death.

He and Florence sitting on the lanai in Hawaii, watching the majestic sunset, feeling the evening warmth, tasting the salty air, and listening to the ageless sound of the crashing waves. She was turned slightly toward him in her chair, holding his hand in hers, her smile communicating that she was right where she wanted to be. The next day, she passed away on the lanai in that same chair.

Ed thought of the change in Pearl's eyes he had watched over the time they had known each other. At first, she looked at him with adoration because she had studied some of his cases in her training and heard many war stories about him. Then as time passed, she would gaze at him like a loving daughter does her father. Her last words in her halted, pained voice last night were, "I love you as a father and a wonderful friend. I'm so glad you came into my life."

The wind gusted hard, again rattling the frozen sliding glass door. Completely iced over, it had turned Ed's little apartment into a cave.

He thought of Florence.

She loved Japanese haiku, poems consisting of 17 syllables in three lines, inspiring images of nature. She had collected them for years, filling a dozen or more spiral notebooks where she wrote, in beautiful calligraphy, her favorites.

"Let me show you one that dates back to my second notebook, ten years ago or so. I could read it to you, but it's important that you read it so you can experience the pauses and amazing word choices.

Ed could only remember the poet's last name, Joso, and that he lived in the 17th century. He remembered the poem, though, because of what Florence said after he read it.

The sleet falls
As if coming through the bottom
Of loneliness.

He read it several times as Florence sat in silence as if wanting him to taste the poem's essence. After a moment, she took his hand and patted it, whispering, "Since you came into my life, Ed, I'm not lonely anymore."

"Florence," he whispered to his empty apartment.

Outside, the storm raged, and Ed closed his eyes, remembering the feel of her hand in his. A single tear rivered down his cheek; he didn't wipe it away.

"Seventy-seven years," he said aloud to the room, "and I've never minded the times I've been alone." He closed his eyes and inhaled raggedly. "Because I never truly was—until now."

He picked up the Glock and held it in his palm. Heavy. Cold.

"*The irony,*" he whispered, thinking of all his years of disliking firearms. He looked at the gun for a long moment, then said it again, "*The irony.*"

He leaned his head against the chair, opened his mouth wide, and lifted the gun.

About The Author

Pearl and Loren

In 1997, Loren began a full-time career as a writer, now with 70 books in print with eight publishers and magazine articles and blog pieces. He edited a police newspaper for seven years. His non-fiction includes books on martial arts, police work, PTSD, mental preparation for violence, meditation, nutrition, exercise, and various subcultures, including prostitution, street gangs, skid row, and the warrior community.

His four-book martial arts fiction series *Dukkha* was a finalist in the prestigious USA Best Book Awards. He has also written novellas, a dozen short stories, and several omnibuses. Three of his books have been best sellers two were considered by Hollywood directors. His work has been published in five languages; four of his books are available in audio at audio.com.

As a martial arts student and teacher since 1965, Loren W. Christensen has earned a 1st-dan black belt in the Filipino fighting art of arnis, a 2nd-degree black belt in aiki jujitsu and, on October 23, 2018, the American Karate Black Belt Association in Lubbock, Texas, awarded him a 10th-dan black belt in American Free Style Karate. Loren was inducted into the master's Hall of Fame in 2011 in Anaheim, California.

Loren began his career in law enforcement in 1967 as a 21-year-old military policeman in the U.S. Army, serving stateside and as a patrolman in Saigon, Vietnam, during the war. At 26, he joined the Portland, Oregon Police Bureau, working various jobs to include street patrol, gang enforcement, intelligence, bodyguarding, and academy trainer, retiring after 25 years.

Other Titles By Loren W. Christensen

The following are available on Amazon, from their publishers, and through the usual book outlets. Signed copies can be purchased at LWC Books, www.lwcbooks.com

Street Stoppers
Fighting In The Clinch
Fighter's Fact Book
Fighter's Fact Book 2
Solo Training **(Bestseller)**
Solo Training 2
Solo Training 3, Over 50
Speed Training
The Fighter's Body
The Mental Edge
The Way Alone
Far Beyond Defensive Tactics
Fighting Power
Crouching Tiger
Anything Goes
Winning With American Kata
Total Defense
Riot
Warriors
On Combat   **(Bestseller)**
Warrior Mindset
Deadly Force Encounters
Deadly Force Encounters, Second Edition
Surviving Workplace Violence
Surviving A School Shooting

Gangbangers
Skinhead Street Gangs
Hookers, Tricks And Cops
Way Of The Warrior
Skid Row Beat
Defensive Tactics
An Introduction to Defensive Tactics For Law Enforcement Officers
Missing Children
Fight Back: Self-Defense For Women
Extreme Joint Locking
Timing In The Martial Arts
Fighter's Guide to Hard-Core Heavy Bag Training
The Brutal Art Of Ripping, Poking And Pressing Vital Targets
How To Live Safely In A Dangerous World
Fighting The Pain Resistant Attacker
Evolution Of Weaponry
Meditation For Warriors
Mental Rehearsal For Warriors
Prostate Cancer
Random Stories
Stupid Crook Stories
Cops' True Stories Of The Paranormal **(Bestseller)**
Seekers of the Paranormal
Policing Saigon
Musings on Violence
Street Lessons, A Journey
Dead Body Calls
Fast Hands

Fiction

Dukkha: The Suffering (Best Books Award Finalist)
Dukkha: Reverb
Dukkha: Unloaded
Dukkha: Hungry Ghosts
Old Ed, Omnibus
Boss, Omnibus
Old Ed 6
Knife Fighter, Omnibus
The Reincarnation of Kato the Monk, novella

The Life and Death of Sensei, novella
Close Encounters of the 7th Kind, novella
Jimmy Long Legs

Short Story Fiction

Old Ed
Old Ed 2
Old Ed 3
Old Ed 4
Old Ed 5
Boss
Boss 2
Boss 3
Parts
Knife Fighter
Knife Fighter 2, novella

DVDs

Solo Training
Fighting Dirty
Speed Training
Masters And Styles
Vital Targets
The Brutal Art Of Ripping, And Pressing Vital Targets

Audio Books

On Combat
Dead Body Calls
Cops' True Stories of the Paranormal
Policing Saigon

You Might Also Like

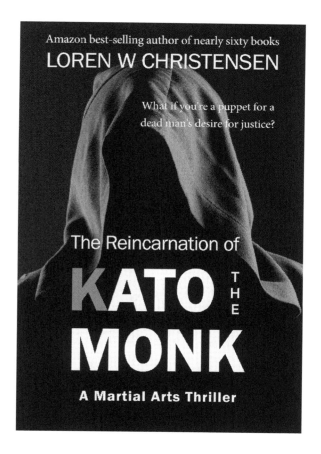

Someone is taking over Kato's mind and body.
Someone called "Mr. Karma."
Someone long dead.

DEAD BODY CALLS

One Street Cop's Experiences with

Homicides
Suicides
Fatal Accidents
Natural Deaths

Foreword by Lt. Col. Dave Grossman

LOREN W. CHRISTENSEN

Best-selling author of 60 books
Co-author of *On Combat* and *Deadly Force Encounters*

"Wow! Delivers from start to finish."
"Loren has been a prolific and brilliant wordsmith."
"This book may be the pinnacle of his craft."
*"While some stories are gruesome, they are told
with respect and professionalism."*

CLOSE ENCOUNTERS OF THE 7TH KIND

a novella

There are seven kinds of encounters humans can have with aliens. The last one is the most controversial and—feared.

WITH BONUS SHORT STORY

PARTS

LOREN W CHRISTENSEN

Best-Selling Author of Cops True Stories of the Paranormal

"If you're a fan of horror definitely check this book out!"
"The author has obviously done his homework on UFOs"
"A powerful masterpiece"

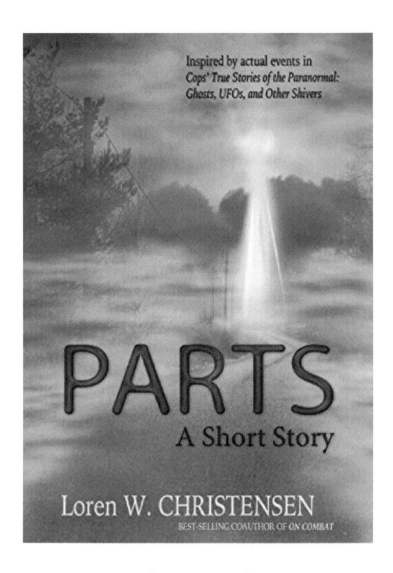

"Wow! Just wow!"
"It gave me a very uncomfortable sense of unease."
"Great story and an incredibly creepy atmosphere."

Note: Parts is available as a stand-alone short story or as a bonus story included with Close Encounters of the 7th Kind

Made in the USA
Columbia, SC
30 March 2023

14515509R00089